my beautiful failure

also by janet ruth young

The Opposite of Music

Things I Shouldn't Think
(previously published as *The Babysitter Murders*)

my beautiful failure

janet ruth young

 ATHENEUM BOOKS FOR YOUNG READERS   New York   London   Toronto   Sydney   New Delhi

ATHENEUM BOOKS FOR YOUNG READERS

An imprint of Simon & Schuster Children's Publishing Division

1230 Avenue of the Americas, New York, New York 10020

This book is a work of fiction. Any references to historical events, real people, or real locales are used fictitiously. Other names, characters, places, and incidents are products of the author's imagination, and any resemblance to actual events or locales or persons, living or dead, is entirely coincidental.

ATHENEUM BOOKS FOR YOUNG READERS is a registered trademark of Simon & Schuster, Inc.

Atheneum logo is a trademark of Simon & Schuster, Inc.

For information about special discounts for bulk purchases, please contact Simon & Schuster Special Sales at 1-866-506-1949 or business@simonandschuster.com.

The Simon & Schuster Speakers Bureau can bring authors to your live event. For more information or to book an event, contact the Simon & Schuster Speakers Bureau at 1-866-248-3049 or visit our website at www.simonspeakers.com.

Book design by Debra Sfetsios-Conover

The text for this book is set in Adobe Caslon.

Manufactured in the United States of America

First Edition

10 9 8 7 6 5 4 3 2 1

Library of Congress Cataloging-in-Publication Data

Young, Janet Ruth, 1957–

My beautiful failure / Janet Ruth Young.

p. cm.

Summary: "While dealing with the recovery of his mentally ill father, sophomore in high school Billy volunteers at a suicide prevention line and falls for one of the incoming callers"— Provided by publisher.

ISBN 978-1-4169-5489-7

ISBN 978-1-4424-4669-4 (eBook)

[1. Hotlines (Counseling)—Fiction. 2. Mental illness—Fiction. 3. Artists—Fiction. 4. Family life—Massachusetts—Fiction. 5. Fathers and sons—Fiction. 6. Massachusetts—Fiction.] I. Title.

PZ7.Y86528My 2012

[Fic]—dc23

2012012572

To volunteers everywhere

Acknowledgments

Thanks to the people who agreed to be interviewed for this book: Lieutenant Kathy Auld and Officer Larry Ingersoll of the Gloucester Police Department, Captain Barry Aptt of the Gloucester Fire Department, Dan Quirk of Beauport Ambulance, Jen Shairs and David Allen, and the painters Ed Touchette and Elynn Kroger. Painter and teacher Susan Guest-McPhail shared her insights with me and reviewed the book for accuracy. Thanks also to my loyal reader/critiquers—Cassandra Oxley, Bridget Rawding, Jan Voogd, and Diane Young. Finally, my appreciation to the people at Atheneum, especially my editor, Ruta Rimas, for their help in shaping and presenting this story.

Courage is what it takes to stand up and speak;
courage is also what it takes to sit down and listen.

—Winston Churchill

PART 1

1.

she was

She was a girl talking to me in the dark.

Everybody knows what happened with my parents. Everybody I talk to when I call.

"You can turn your life around," I had told her. "Starting today, you can be free. You can do anything you want. Don't you see that?"

I'm down, but I'm not out. I'm a fighter. On my good days, few can defeat me.

"I admire that about you," I had told her.

I remember every compliment you ever gave me. Especially when you said I was strong.

"I have to go. Will you be okay?"

I'll handle it. I always do. Good night, sweet Hallmark prince.

2.

new directions

"Where is everyone?" Dad asked when he got home. It was October 25, and he had just come from his therapy appointment. Dad looked good these days, like someone who had a purpose. He shaved in the morning and dressed for work in a jacket and tie and Rockport loafers. He stood straighter and was no longer bony. His felty red hair was cut short, so that it verged on stylish, and he wore a sharp, arrowlike goatee. He worked as a draftsman at Liberty Fixtures, a company that made shelving for department stores. He looked a lot like me, if I were fifty and had accepted that I would always hate the job I needed.

I was just in from a bike ride. Mom and Linda were making pizza and salad for supper. Dad dropped a bag marked ART SUPPLIES on the dining room table. You could hear the rush-hour traffic going by out back; the highway ran right behind our house.

Drive past our house: the bright orange door, the brass

knocker in the shape of a salamander (unnecessary because we have a functioning doorbell), our name and house number (Morrison 32) painted in black Gothic lettering on a white rock at the end of the driveway—that's all Linda's work. And Mom directed a museum. We might as well have a sign outside saying Artistic People Live Here. Right now Linda and Mom were laying the pepperoni slices in overlapping circles to look like a chrysanthemum. The art supplies could have been for almost anyone—anyone but me.

"I'm going to paint again," Dad said. He looked quietly fierce, like a gladiator before the lion is let out.

"Yippee!" Linda danced around, wriggling and elfish. She switched from teenager mode to little girl mode when she wanted to feel closer to my parents.

Mom dried her hands and wrapped her arms around Dad's middle.

"That's exciting, honey. But you've always painted."

"I mean get *serious* about painting. I want to be in the art world again. I put my art aside. Because of the needs of making a living and raising a family."

Excuse me for being born, I thought.

"That's a sad story," Linda said. Linda's style reworked droopy clothes that had belonged to an elderly person, which made her look younger than thirteen. She came up to Dad's armpit, and she had a wormy way of sharing his space. Now she slipped her hand into Dad's, and he held it in the air like it was a prize. I was as tall as he was, so he never looked at me, or my hand, that way.

"I never stopped you," Mom said. "I never told you you couldn't paint." Like Linda, Mom worked to separate herself from the run of humanity. She wore her black hair perfectly straight, wore dark lipstick, and owned only necklaces that were one of a kind. Usually they were made for her by someone noteworthy, such as a blind sculptor, a poetry-writing shepherd, or a male nun.

"Of course not, sweetie," Dad said. He crinkled his eyes at Mom, like he was winking to make her admit a lie.

"Don't forget, Bill, I fell in love with you over *Inverted Horizon*."

"I'm not forgetting."

Inverted Horizon was the ocean-on-top sunset painting of Dad's that was shown by a Fifty-Seventh Street gallery in New York City when Mom was in graduate school and Dad was working at a paint store. He ended up selling that to a collector, as well as his vertical sunset painting *Perpendicular Horizon*. He once told me that they were the best things he had ever done—part technical exercise, part making fun of the sunset cliché, and part, he said, "Just something great to look at."

At the opening reception, Mom stood in front of *Inverted Horizon* for a long time. A tall guy in an army fatigue jacket and tuxedo pants came along and stood beside her, and without his saying anything, she knew he was the painter. Although I don't like to view either of my parents as a love object, I always felt that was a good way to meet someone: nothing flashy or obvious, just a meeting of the minds and a sense of being immediately understood.

"Well, for the record," Mom continued, "I completely support your painting. As of today, as of right now, and for the future. Completely."

"I completely do too, Dad." Linda scurried away from Dad and emptied the bag: tubes of paint, brushes, brush cleaner.

"Why all of a sudden?" I asked, leaning on one end of the table. I didn't touch Dad or his art supplies. I knew enough to see that he had about three hundred dollars' worth.

"Dr. Fritz and I talked about it. Art is my missing piece." Dad pointed to the paints, then tapped a spot somewhere between his heart and his gut. "The missing piece of my emotional puzzle."

"Are you sure this is a good idea?" I finally said.

"Why not?" he asked. A distinctive painting of a chicken, done by someone at Mom's museum, hung on one wall. Anytime people came for dinner, they commented on the chicken. Dad's gaze drifted to it, then back to me. A year ago he fit into my clothes. Now he had put weight on, even had a little belly forming.

"I would hate to see you get all excited and set yourself up . . ."

"Set myself up?" Dad pressed. Was he challenging me to say it?

"He's fine now, Billy," Mom said.

Dad spoke at the same time. "I painted thirty years ago."

"I don't want you to get too involved in it and then get upset. That's all."

"What would upset me? And even so, why can't I get upset?"

Mom and Linda wouldn't say it. But I didn't want a repeat of last winter.

last winter: a memory

I've brought a new friend home after school. It's only two thirty, and I see Dad's car in the driveway. He must have come home early. I walk into the living room with my friend, expecting to introduce him to Dad. Gordon is so superb that I really want to impress him. He's new in town, and though some of the other new kids are snobby, Gordon isn't. He plays French horn and has played on the White House lawn with the All-State band. He seems confident and relaxed in every situation, and his hair seems exactly the same length every time I see him.

I hear Dad moving at the other end of the house, and call his name. In the past he's always had a story or joke for my friends. Sometimes he's played an aria from his collection of opera CDs. But this time he doesn't come.

"Just a minute," I tell Gordon. Finally Dad walks into the hall, but he doesn't look at Gordon or me. He goes past us, toward the den, rubbing his hands and whistling tunelessly. Now he's coming back again.

"Dad, stop a minute. I want you to meet someone."

"Are you looking for something, Mr. Morrison?" Gordon asks. "Can I help you find it?"

Gordon watches Dad with that game smile: relaxed, confident. But I begin to realize that Dad's walking and his whistling are involuntary, that some kind of worry is driving Dad from one end of the house to the other.

After a few minutes Gordy also realizes something is very wrong, something I haven't told him because I didn't know and I wouldn't know how to explain it if I did. He walks back to the bus stop with his instrument case and his backpack, and that is the last time I bring a friend home.

4.

last winter: what happened

Dad stopped sleeping, then eating, then working, then talking. I can tell you how long it lasted because I counted the days: 128. October to March.

what mom did

When Dad got better, Mom's boss at the Brooksbie Museum resigned, and Mom practically moved in. Mom was director now, and she could ask the other workers, even the unpaid ones, to do more than they wanted, the way Pudge had asked her. She was all about the museum, dedicated to the history of the Massachusetts leather industry, with rarely a sentence about anything else. Her promotion became a shiny new scooter, her guilt about what happened to Dad the Mom-style sneakers that propel her forward. When I questioned her she said, "He's fine now." When I questioned her further she added, "Isn't he?" and went back to reviewing slides for the museum.

In the summer the four of us went camping in two tents beside a New Hampshire lake, and Mom and Dad told Linda and me, while we sealed cheese sandwiches in foil and dropped them into the fire, that the trip was to thank us for our help over the winter. After that we didn't say "depression" anymore. We mostly said "last winter."

blanks

The day after Dad decided to paint again, I watched from the front door as his car pulled up. He unloaded twelve canvases from the trunk. That must have set him back two hundred dollars.

Linda and her friend Jodie burst impishly from the house. Jodie was pale and soft, with flimsy hair that was always shedding its ornaments. Jodie had the backbone of a ramen noodle. She did everything Linda did. I suppose if Linda ever died, Jodie wouldn't be able to give the eulogy because she will have died too. Most of her time was spent doing crafts at our house: pounding brown leaves in the bathtub and calling them paper, or baking clay poops in the oven and calling them ceramics.

Dad had the girls carry the canvases into the utility room right off the driveway—a (strangely) underutilized room that housed our furnace and some sports equipment, cleaning supplies, and tools.

"What's the plan?" Linda asked, stepping over some cross-country ski poles.

"This is going to be my studio," Dad said. He pulled the chain on a light above his head. "I'm going to actualize every major idea I've had since leaving art school."

"A studio," Jodie said. She stacked the canvases against one wall. "I love the sound of that."

"That seems ambitious, Dad."

"Billy. I didn't see you there." I had followed them in. I was wearing socks without shoes, and my feet made no sound.

"'Ambitious' is no longer a dirty word in my life," Dad said. "It was for a while. And I'm sorry if it is in yours. If so, that's my fault, because I haven't shown you what's important."

Dad's ancient suitcase, full of miscellaneous small hardware pieces, sat on an old table that had belonged to Grandma Pearl. I loved running my hands through the pieces when I was little. The churning metal made the same sound as beach stones being rolled back and forth by a wave.

"I'm ambitious, Dad," I said, rumpling the metal for old times' sake. It wasn't like Dad, the old Dad anyway, to be so serious and to speak in long paragraphs. I didn't get why everything he said these days had to have such a *point* to it.

He motioned to me to move the suitcase to the floor. "How are your grades? Are they ambitious grades?" he asked.

Jodie made an O at Linda, as if they had caught me getting yelled at.

"I told you, they'll be up. I have high hopes for this year. I just need to get focused." I hadn't told my parents, but school was for me like Dad's job was for him: the thing I needed but hated.

Dad slid a stepstool from beneath the old table. He reached for a shelf set high into the wall and pulled out a heavy box. As the box came forward it tipped, but Dad caught it.

"God, look at all this," he said, taking out old sketches, textbooks, and photographs. A few framed paintings were in the stack as well. He brought down more boxes, and Linda and Jodie piled them near the cleared-out space by the canvases.

"I want to see what's in these," Linda said.

"We want to see everything," Jodie added.

"No." Dad closed the boxes, and his voice got low. "I'll go through these on my own. Lots of good memories here. You girls go back to what you were doing. Thank you."

I pretended to help organize until the girls were gone.

"A studio," I said, pressing my back against the door as Dad cleared out some beach toys that could go into the attic. "How about just doing one or two paintings to see whether you still like it? A few months ago you were just getting back into normal life. You couldn't even . . ."

Dad froze. I didn't know how to talk to him without being offensive. I hoped he'd see that I was trying to help, just like Linda and Jodie had been. I stuffed my hands into the cuffs of my sweater, as if they were the words I needed to take back. How could I say it? There was a past him and a present him, and he didn't agree with me on which him he was.

When he spoke again he didn't look angry. He seemed understanding—tender almost, the kind of understanding that makes you feel small and stupid.

"You were a big help last year, Billy. We both know you and Mom and Linda nearly saved my life. But please don't treat me like I'm still sick. Because if you treat me like I'm sick, I'll start acting like I'm sick, and then the next thing you know I will be sick. And I don't ever want to be sick again."

"That's exactly what I don't want, Dad." *I should touch him*, I thought. *Just go ahead and do it, the way Linda does.* I pulled my hand out and aimed it toward Dad's shoulder.

He caught my hand in midair, like I was high-fiving him. He clasped my fingers and pressed them back to me.

"Here's an idea, Billy," Dad said, pulling out some rags to wipe the plaster dust from his old portfolio. The way he touched that old stuff. As if he could feel the years dried up inside it. As if he could add water and his college days would spring back to life. "You have a lot of talent. Why don't you find a project of your own?"

7 .

private beach

Choose your poison," Gordon said, leading me to the wicker papasan chairs on his deck overlooking a private beach. Gordy's father was a lawyer and they were rich, but Gordy would never lord it over anyone. He held out two pints of ice cream: pistachio and peanut butter cup. Premium, of course. I liked both and would have preferred to share, but not knowing if rich people shared ice cream, I took pistachio. He transferred his to a bowl, so I did the same.

"He thinks I need a project," I explained. We'd started this conversation on the phone, but I wanted some privacy and would use any excuse to visit.

"What did your mom say?"

"She agreed with him."

"Ouch. I can see why you're ticked off."

I watched an airplane drop expertly over the Boston skyline and into Logan Airport.

"But you know, it's kind of reasonable," Gordy said.

"It is?"

14

"Well, maybe he means not that you're in the way, which is how you're taking it, but that you should have something you're really excited about. Because he's excited about something, and it's cool to be excited. Do you want to try the peanut butter cup, too? I have a couple of extra spoons."

We switched flavors, but I was too distracted to form an opinion on which I liked better.

"You must have good parents to want to put that kind of spin on what parents say. I mean, you must have had—" I felt awkward around Gordy every time I said "parents," plural. His mother died of cystic fibrosis shortly after they came to town. The main thing people knew about Gordy, for months and months, was that his mom had coughed blood into a handkerchief in the administrative office when she registered him for school.

"Tell me this," Gordy said after swallowing what was in his mouth and wiping his lips with a napkin. "What do you like to do?"

"You know. Ride my bike, listen to music." I tick-tocked the spoon to show how monotonous I was.

"What about your songwriting? Are you still doing that?"

"Yeah, but it feels empty. Everything is flat. I mean, last year—last year felt so important. I saved somebody's life, you know? What could be more important than that? I don't know what to do other than take longer and longer bike rides." I put down my ice cream and slouched in the chair, arms folded across my chest. "I'm only sixteen, and I feel like my life is over.

"I guess it's different for you," I continued. "You have

Brenda. Someone you can tell your hopes and dreams to. Someone who knows everything about you and thinks you're amazing."

"Whoa! Let's not go overboard. She thinks I'm okay. I don't remember her using the word 'amazing.'"

"She's a great catch," I insisted.

Gordon chuckled. "Remember when Brenda and I went to the Roomful of Blues concert? Mitchell was in line waiting for their tickets. Andy was out on the sidewalk trying to chat up some girl, and every time he looked at Brenda and me he would say, 'Nice work' or 'Major score' or 'You the man.' I had to tell him to cut it out because he was making Brenda uncomfortable."

"The other girl too, probably. What a jerk."

Gordy wagged his spoon at me. "I know what your project should be," he said.

"What?"

He looked into his ice cream to make his suggestion seem nonchalant. "Why don't you join the Listeners?"

"The people with that big sign over the bridge?" I sat upright and Gordy laughed. I hadn't expected this at all.

"The suicide hotline. According to the sign, they're always looking for people. They even want people our age. Actually, I've thought of you every time I've seen that sign."

I had seen the sign, of course, but never connected it to myself. Never connected it to any real person. But certainly there were people on the other end, taking the calls. Gordy was even more exceptional than I had given him credit for. "That seems like it would be important. Talking somebody off a ledge."

"You'd be great at it," Gordy said, piling all that remained of both flavors into my bowl. "And you have the experience to back it up. If I ever got so low I wanted to off myself, you'd be the first person I'd call."

research

Back in my room, I looked up the Listeners' website. A video on their homepage showed cars driving over the Joseph E. Garland Bridge, under the Listeners sign. Someone got out of his car and walked to the railing. He saw the Listeners sign that said FEELING DESPERATE? CALL US NOW. Steady piano chords, ominous, like the tolling of a bell, played over the scene. Then the video switched to a youngish woman. She said she had lost her job and apartment and her kids were about to be taken from her, and she had been in so much pain that it hurt her to live each day. She'd put on a parka with big pockets and driven to the beach to fill those pockets with rocks. She'd been about to walk into the water and drown herself, but as she pulled into the beach parking lot she called the Listeners number and they talked her out of it.

"Without Listeners I wouldn't be here," she said, "and my kids wouldn't have a mother."

Another guy talked about how his sister had killed

herself and he had felt helpless to stop it. I was glad I had my earbuds on. I wouldn't want Mom and Dad to hear.

A college student came on next. The caption beneath her picture said "Volunteer Coordinator." "This is a life-saving service," she said. "People call us who can't talk to anyone else. When they call here, they can break out of their isolation and be themselves. Finally they have a connection to someone and something." As the music got louder, she looked directly at the camera—at me, I felt—and said, "We save lives every day."

The last shot was a line from the sign: VOLUNTEERS WANTED.

Gordy was right. This organization was perfect for me. I had so much saving to give. I only needed someone who wanted to be saved.

I went into the living room, where Dad was studying his art books in happy silence, with not even an opera CD to distract him. I felt completely invisible compared with his revived interest in painting.

The living room was all white, accented by Mom's humorous throw pillows with sayings like WELL-BEHAVED WOMEN RARELY MAKE HISTORY and WHAT WOULD LADY GODIVA DO? In fact, in its own way, our living room resembled a book.

"I found my project," I said. It sounded like I was throwing that at him, accusing him of something. "Dad, I found my project," I said again. I clapped my hand over my chest. *I* had a project. *Even I.*

"What are you going to do?" He closed the book, with one finger inside to hold his page.

"I'm going to volunteer on a hotline."

"Like a phone line?" Dad asked. "Where?"

"The Listeners. You've seen their sign on the bridge." I might have said more, but I couldn't say "depression" or "suicide" in front of Dad. Maybe because those words made Dad look weak, and maybe because hearing those words might give Dad ideas and he might off himself. It would be good, anyway, to work in a place where those words could be said out loud.

"Where would you do this? Here at the house?"

"In their office downtown."

"They take sixteen-year-olds as volunteers?"

"Most of their volunteers are high school and college students." I liked the college-student angle. If I worked with Hawthorne State students, I would be more mature than other high school guys, a sort of tweener.

Dad closed his book and folded his hands over it. He smiled, and because I hadn't seen him smile a lot lately, I felt like he was laughing at me.

"Billy," he said, "when I said you should have a project, I thought maybe you and Gordy might form a band."

"Meaning?" I hooked my hands on the loops of my jeans to make me stand prouder, although I didn't feel it.

"That job sounds like a huge responsibility."

"That's why I want it," I said. "Because it's more important than starting a band. Besides, a French horn and a harmonica are not much of a band."

Mom came in with her reading glasses and *New England Journal of History*. "What's important?"

"Billy wants to get involved with the Listeners," Dad told her. "The hotline people."

"They're—" I began to explain.

"I know who they are," Mom said, sitting down. "That doesn't seem like a great idea. I'm not saying you wouldn't be good at it—I know you would—but it seems a little morbid. I don't know that I'd want to be listening to people's problems hour after hour. Plus, they're kind of a rival of ours."

"In what sense?" Dad asked. They enjoyed this kind of conversation—the kind that started with me, then drifted away from me.

"They and the museum tend to go after the same money."

Parents have a way of getting calmer and calmer that makes you more and more upset. I spoke so emphatically now that I leaned forward with each word. "I want to *help people*! I want to do something that isn't a *waste of time*!" As soon as the words were out of my mouth I wondered if Dad thought this was a dig at his painting. If he thought so, he didn't react.

"Will you have adult supervision?" Mom asked. "I wouldn't have a clue what to say if someone called up and said they were, uh . . ."

I would beat them at their own game. I made my voice sound bored, as if I were working at Listeners already. "They have a trainer there all the time. They have a program that you follow. You don't just make up what you say. Look, their website says they're desperate for people. I should at least go meet them and see what they say."

"Give it a try," Dad said finally. "But don't let it get to you, okay? Don't be a hero. If it gets too stressful, tell Mom and me. And don't hesitate to walk out of there and do something that someone your age would consider fun."

9.

headquarters

Command Central for the Listeners was in a secret location in downtown Hawthorne, on the third floor of Cabot Hall, home of the Cabot Insurance Company, which lent two rooms to the organization rent free. Despite the big billboard on the bridge, no sign on Cabot Hall betrayed what went on here. When I arrived for my training I found a dingy office with sticky floors, cockroaches that darted around in my peripheral vision, and the stale aroma of forgotten falafel. The college guy who opened the door for me said the grit made the place more authentic. Maybe he believed all the suicidal callers must live with sticky floors too. But I assumed Cabot Insurance used the secrecy as an excuse not to send their cleaning people upstairs.

On the walls I saw more versions of the Listeners poster, each one with a black-and-white photo of a face turned three-quarters away from the camera. These people were supposed to represent our core constituency: depressed, distraught, discouraged, and in some cases ready to throw in the towel. But the faces looked like professional models, and they didn't seem all that depressed to me. One looked like he was waiting for the mail. Another looked like she could use a forty-four-ounce cola. If Listeners wanted a true representation of mental anguish, they should bring in some paintings. Dad once told me the most anguished paintings were Edvard Munch's *The Scream* and Van Gogh's *Wheatfield with Crows*.

The person in charge of training was named Pep; her full name was Amalia "Pepper" Salton. I was impressed that her nickname had a nickname. Pep's father was a congressman and a Listeners trustee. He raised piles of money for the organization. Pep was a junior in college, and she looked like a tennis player, along the lines of Dad's work friend June Melman, except that June's posture was exemplary and Pep had a to-hell-with-it slouch. She wore a white blouse with the collar turned up and a navy headband. Seeing Pep reminded me of all I liked about June, whom I had a crush on last year—her white-blond hair, her cream-colored warmup suit, her scent of expensive lotions, but most of all, that she jogged the whole route beside our runaway bus of last winter. In another time and place, I would have done anything for June.

In the front room of Listeners, two guys with beards discussed a hockey game, and a girl with heavy black-framed glasses read a thick chemistry book. Pep explained that although many of the Listeners were college students who needed to fulfill a community-service requirement in order to graduate, I wouldn't be working the phone bank with them. College kids like these were fairly independent, she said. They were allowed to work the phones alone if necessary, and sometimes they stayed on and took calls right through the night. But since I was in high school, I would be in the teen room, working limited hours with two ListMates who would show me the ropes.

She led me to one end of a long table with three telephones and three metal chairs. At the other end was Margaret, a girl in a plaid school uniform who might have been sixteen like me. In the middle was Richie, who looked fourteen. Who was he qualified to counsel? My sister, Linda?

Right away, I was irritated by the age segregation. So the two bearded guys and the chem major were in college. What did age really mean in the grand scheme of things? After all, I had been through what I'd been through. My application included a short essay about all the ways I helped Dad last winter. The other three had— what, taken the SATs, been rejected by a few schools, and learned to operate the juicer at Orange Julius? I smiled collegially at my teen peers, but I kept getting stuck on that fourteen-year-old.

Pep told me I needed to learn the ground rules. She handed me my training booklet, *The Four Pillars of Listening*.

1. WHAT HAPPENS AT LISTENERS STAYS AT LISTENERS. All phone calls that come in are confidential. We discuss them only with other Listeners, not with anyone outside.

No exceptions, ever, period. We exchange first names with the people who call, and because we don't use caller ID or track calls, we'll never know their full names, phone numbers, or where they live, and they will never know ours. We're not their friend, and we don't develop any kind of ongoing relationship with them. Your involvement with the person begins with the call and ends with the call. In fact, if someone you know calls, you should not acknowledge that you recognize them. That would be a violation of the Incoming's privacy.

I asked what an Incoming was, and Richie, a blond curl bobbing knowledgeably on his forehead, told me an Incoming is the person who calls.

Pep pushed up her sleeve to reveal a thick gold watch. She explained that Listeners had special terms for certain things and that I would have to learn the lingo.

I felt stupid, because I should have been able to figure out what an Incoming was. I decided not to ask many questions, in case they thought I wasn't bright enough to do the job.

2. IT'S NOT ABOUT YOU. Always keep the conversation focused on the Incoming. Do not reveal any personal information about yourself. Don't tell the Incomings anything about your experiences, problems,

or preferences. Do not give advice. You don't necessarily know any more about solving their problems than they do. Just listen to them and reflect what they're saying.

Margaret waved her hand between us as if we were role-playing a phone conversation. She told me that the best way to respond to the Incoming was to be like a mirror: Repeat what they've already said, even using the same words. She said that this might feel awkward, but it would let the Incoming know that I was really listening.

3. ENTER THEIR WORLD. Never question the reality of your Incomings. If they say they're royalty, believe them. If they say they're the leader of special forces in Afghanistan, believe them. If they say they woke up this morning and discovered they were living in the middle of a spiderweb, believe them.

Margaret told me that one Incoming actually did believe he was living in a spiderweb.

Richie chimed in that it helped to think of each person as a different planet. For instance, if Jason called with the spiderweb thing, I should tell myself that I was living on the Jason Planet and that was okay.

4. ALWAYS ASK (ALWAYS!). Listeners is in the business of suicide prevention. You must ask each Incoming whether he or she

is feeling suicidal. If the Incoming says yes, follow the procedure for urging the Incoming to call the police or a hospital. But if the Incoming doesn't give you permission to call emergency services, there is nothing you can do.

I flinched as if I'd been paintballed in the face. This I could not believe. Nothing we could do? A suicidal person is on the line and we're supposed to just hang up? I asked if this was because we had no addresses or phone numbers. Margaret said that was right: We had no records, no last names, no nothing. Just a voice on the phone.

rule number 4

Margaret asked if I was all right. She said I looked like I had stopped breathing.

I told her I'd felt fine until rule number 4. I rested my hand on one of the phones as if to test myself. The job was monumental, the ultimate responsibility. The way the rules were written, someday someone might call and mine would be the last voice that person would ever hear. In a few days I would start saving lives. But only if they wanted to be saved.

I talked with my teen mentors for a few more minutes. Then I rode home with the booklet in one hand, curled around the handlebars. As I reached the driveway I stashed the booklet in my pack. I liked having a booklet no one in my family was allowed to read. It was my book of secrets.

in my corner

Back home, Mom was working on the high-end laptop she inherited when she became Brooksbie director.

"How was it?" she asked as I walked into the all-white living room.

"Excellent," I said.

"Did you save anyone?"

"Not yet," I told her. I carried my bike, Triumph, across the carpet and into my room. Rolling the bike across the white rug was definitely verboten.

"I know you, Billy," Mom called. She had closed her laptop on the big square coffee table and curled her bare feet up into the chair. "You don't look happy. What's wrong?"

"The place seems great. It's just that even though I have real-life experience they grouped me with the other high school students rather than the older volunteers."

"This is an important life lesson, Billy," she said. "Do you know what you're going to have to do?"

"Threaten to quit?" I asked, stuffing the manual into my back pocket.

"*Au contraire*, my friend. This is no time to be a hothead." She took off her reading glasses. I've been planning to hole up in my room, but this show of interest made me stop.

"But I already know I'm good at helping people. I don't deserve this treatment."

"You're going to have to check that attitude at the door."

"How can I?"

Mom laughed. She reached up and poked me. For a self-described bohemian, she had an oddly cheerleaderish side.

"Because of your age, you're going to have to work twice as hard as the others to prove yourself. It's the same way for women and people of color. Now that I have Pudge's files I have some inkling as to how much work he had to do to stay where he was."

"Half?" I asked, pulling up an ottoman to sit closer to Mom. This arrangement of couches and chairs Mom called the "conversation area," and here Mom and I were, having our own conversation.

"That's right. Half as much as I did as assistant director, even when I worked a reduced schedule last winter.

"Pudge had a lot of great ideas," Mom continued, "but he left things half finished. It's like some deity came along, plucked him from his desk at the Brooksbie, and lifted him, with clouds and angel choirs, to a perfect job at the Museum of New England Heritage. And did he worry about leaving a mess? No, he just declared victory and moved on. But some people are like that, never dotting the i's or crossing the t's. Our family has the opposite problem: We try too hard sometimes."

Mom was right. We tried everything to make Dad better, from antidepressants to nutritional supplements to light therapy. It had been a winter of dotting all our vowels.

"Gggggg!"

Linda stood in the hall, listening to our conversation.

"Get out of here, Linda," I say. "Mom and I are having a serious conversation about work."

"Linda, this isn't the time," Mom said.

"Gggggg," Linda warbled.

"That's enough, Linda," said Mom, raking the earpiece of her glasses through her hair, a sign that she was annoyed. "Ignore your sister, Billy. Remember that what doesn't kill you makes you stronger. Every kick is a boost."

"Did they work you too hard at the Listerines?" Linda threw her head forward. "Guuuuuuuuugggh."

"Gigigigigig." Jodie was beside her, gargling at a high pitch, so that they made harmony. They wore matching Justin Bieber nightshirts.

"It's nine thirty," I complained. "What's she doing here? Mom, don't tell me she's sleeping over."

"No wonder you're so exhausted," Linda said, widening her eyes and sounding like a sympathetic adult. "How many life-threatening cases of bad breath did you cure today?"

Jodie tried to look serious but then crumpled. She laughed so hard, she couldn't even gargle.

"Cut it out! Both of you!" I pushed the ottoman back to the wall. My great private moment with Mom was shattered.

"I'm sorry, Billy," Jodie said. "But Linda's so funny. She cracks me up and I can't help it."

"Do you need to borrow a toothbrush, Jodie?" Linda put a hand on Jodie's shoulder like she was showing her around the house. "Do you want a glass or some mouthwash?"

"What brand do you have?" Jodie asked as they left.

"So what do people say when they call?" Mom asked.

"I haven't started on the phones yet. But when I do I won't tell you anything." I mimed zipping my lip. I would stop there and leave her hanging. I went into my room with the handbook and closed the door.

12.

wrong with you

I leaned against my headboard, under my two Escher prints, and looked again at the Listeners handbook. In addition to the four rules, they had provided sample conversations I could practice with. It seemed like a good organization. They had thought through every possibility, and aside from seating me with Margaret and Richie, they showed a lot of trust by putting me on the phones.

I pulled out my copy of *Your Mental Health: A Layman's Guide to the Psychiatrist's Bible*, by Allen Frances and Michael B. First. It was like a big catalogue of all the things that can go wrong with a person's mind. Mom had bought it for me for my last birthday, after I decided I would eventually become a psychologist. Mom hated doctors because when Grandma Pearl got cancer, the doctors kept treating her for way too long and wouldn't let her die. So you might have thought she would shun my ambition. But she liked knowing that this subject would place me on a rigorous university track. And she was big on prestige.

She would like seeing my name with two, three, even five letters after it. She would fondle my letters like jewels on a Mom necklace.

For now I just enjoyed browsing and matching people I knew with the illnesses explained in the book. Mom's uncle Jack, for instance, who hid from everybody when he returned from World War II: *post-traumatic stress disorder.* Dad's old tennis partner, Richard Bramble, who did time for stealing from a sporting-goods store and then set up a fictional investment company to rip off old people: *kleptomania* and *antisocial personality disorder.* Uncle Marty's former business partner at his bar/restaurant, who got so mad during an argument over the bookkeeping that he broke every glass in the place: *intermittent explosive disorder.* I also read the descriptions of the illnesses we heard about most in high school: *substance abuse, substance dependence, substance-induced delirium*, and the fat and thin eating disorders. The pages about Dad's illness, *major depressive disorder with psychotic features*, were full of my notes and underlinings.

It would have been tempting to use this book at Listeners, even to show it to Margaret and Richie. But the booklet said to think of our Incomings as individuals: living, breathing people with unique sets of problems, who were almost friends but not our friends, and never an agglomeration of illnesses.

13.

they are your friends

I found a roll of Life Savers on my school lunch tray.

"For you," my friend Mitchell said, bowing slightly at the waist, enough to dent his rotund shape. "Gordy told us that you are a Life Saver now. Life Savers: The Candy with the Hole, Registered Trademark."

"Or," Andy said, "just call him Hole for short."

"I am not going to call him Hole for short," Mitchell replied. "For short I will call him Registered Trademark, or R."

I was pleased at first, but now it was clear I was being laughed at. "I don't want your candy," I told Mitchell. "Not if you're not being serious."

"That's right," Gordy added. "You guys aren't funny. I think what Billy is doing is admirable. I didn't want to set him up to be ridiculed." This was a perfect example of why I wasn't close to Mitchell anymore. Only Gordy knew anything about last winter. Mitchell I never told, and Andy was Mitchell's friend, not mine. I'd known

36

Mitchell all my life (we were born on the same day) and I once valued his knack for making anything seem funny or stupid. When Dad got sick that knack held no value for me. Now Andy had become Mitchell's acolyte. Andy was a short wrestler with a head shaped like a fire hydrant. He also loved ridiculing people but wasn't quite as good at it as Mitchell.

"Thanks, Gord," I said.

I moved down the table, leaving two seats between Mitchell and me. I focused on my lunch, the cafeteria's signature dish of American chop suey. The class of 2005, spearheaded by a group of vegetarians, had decorated the cafeteria with murals of fruits and vegetables, Godzilla-like bananas and gargantuan heads of romaine, but the caf didn't serve many of those things. What they did dish up was some form of ground beef, every day.

"All right, then. If you don't want them." Andy peeled back the foil wrapper.

"Hey!" I jumped up and knocked Andy's arm.

"You're not gonna share?" he asked.

"I'll share. I just want to be the one to open it."

"That's mature," Mitchell said, toasting me with a bottle of chocolate milk.

Maybe I had no sense of humor. But I had volunteered. I went to the training and I studied the handbook. And now I wasn't entitled to all fourteen pieces of candy?

"Thank you, R," Mitchell said, taking a pineapple Life Saver. He nudged Andy with his elbow. "Can you stop that?"

Andy was licking his index finger to pick up the shreds

of cheese that had fallen off his burrito. "I think I'd get sick of helping people," he said. "I'd be, like, can't you help yourselves?"

"I don't get this whole offing-yourself business," Mitchell said after belching soundlessly. "I'm planning to hang on for as long as possible. I think it's entirely likely that during our lifetime the technology will be developed that will allow us to live forever. Maybe in the next ten, twenty years. Why miss out on that just because—what, you lost your money in the stock market or something?"

I tilted my head and stared at Mitchell. People who've never suffered have a young-seeming stupidity that makes them all alike. Mitchell didn't know how little it took to start someone on the path Dad walked last winter. In fact, although Dad's doctor offered some theories, we were never entirely sure why Dad became depressed. I confided in Gordy about Dad all along because I knew Gordy had also suffered. Gordy was one of the few people my age who could understand me. People who've suffered can think alike, even if their sufferings are different.

"Those people will be sorry," Andy said. "May I have my dessert now?"

"Sure," I said, because Andy had so little going for him.

"Don't pick through them, Andy," Mitchell said. "Just take the first one in the roll."

"I don't entirely get it either," Gordy added. He had finished his sandwich and was balling up the foil. He brought his lunch every day, and it was better than what the cafeteria served. He didn't stint on the flourishes and extras. Today it had been turkey on a bulkie roll with stuffing and cranberry sauce. "Not that I'm the happiest person in the world. I just put a lot of faith in getting out of bed every morning."

"If you ask me, a lot of suicidal people are only being dramatic," said Mitchell. He nodded toward the corner of the cafeteria where Heidi Destino was sitting. She swallowed a whole bottle of aspirin after Rick Byers dumped her for Melissa Foley, and then Heidi called everybody in town saying that she was going to die and Rick was the only one who could save her. He rushed to her house and drove her to the emergency room—carried her through the automatic door in his arms, someone said—and sat beside her, crying, while her stomach was pumped. Then they got back together, and Melissa Foley, though cuter, became the odd man out, because Heidi almost acted as though she had a weird power over Rick. Now Rick looked upset all the time, and I heard he had started praying a lot and had even gone back to church. And Melissa, she just looked baffled, as if to say, *How do you compete with that?*

"Was your old school as drama infested as this?" I asked Gordy.

"Not really." He took a blackberry Life Saver. "At my old school all anyone cared about was getting into the right college. I think the suicide attempts came later."

"Okay, Dr. Billy," Mitchell said, adjusting his suspenders, as he always did after lunch. "I can't wait until you're a real psychiatrist and pulling down the big bucks. I'll be your first patient. If I can afford you."

"What about me?" Andy asked. "I won't have to pay

you, right? You'll see me for free, right? If I need to discuss my dreams or girls or anything."

"I believe those two subjects will always be discussed in close conjunction," Mitchell said, standing up.

The bell rang. "Speaking of two subjects in close conjunction," Andy said, "Bren-Bren has a new sweater." Gordy frowned at Andy so hard that his chin dimpled, then pretended to dump him out of his chair. Brenda Mason was waving from the other side of the caf.

"Actually, Mitchell and Andy both think it's pretty cool what you're doing," Gordy said as he and I walked toward Brenda. "Though Andy's thinking of calling the line and pretending to be standing on a ledge when you answer the phone. He's been practicing a different voice and everything. People just find it easier to make fun of things like death."

I wasn't sure what to say. When Gordy's mother died, for a while it made him seem holy, like he had entered and exited a private chamber few people our age have visited. Since I saw no flaws in his personality or the way he behaved toward people, I wouldn't diagnose him with anything but missing his mother: maybe *adjustment disorder* or PTSD. Mitchell thought he was smarter than everyone around him, which could be a form of *narcissistic personality disorder*. Andy had trouble forming his own opinions and relied on Mitchell for everything he knew, which sounded like *dependent personality disorder*.

Brenda said hi to me before taking off with Gordy. She had wavy dark hair and indoor-pale skin. She was one of the smartest and nicest girls in school, but some of her pants were so tight I thought her skeleton might start complaining. (Overemphasis on physical appearance: *histrionic personality disorder?*)

I offered Brenda a Life Saver. Five gone, nine left for me. I slid the roll deep in my pocket and gave it a protective pat.

14.

the art world

That night Dad tried another take on the sunset theme he'd had success with thirty years ago. At nine o'clock Mom and Linda went into the utility room, now called the studio, to check on his progress. At eleven thirty the rest of us went to bed. At one o'clock I got up for a drink of apple juice and saw the light still on in Dad's studio.

I tapped on the door, then pushed. Offenbach's *Tales of Hoffman* played softly on a paint-spattered CD player. In front of his easel, Dad swayed to "Barcarolle."

"I forgot how good I was at this," he told me. His smile was one of a younger time. I had never seen it in person, only in his wedding picture. The small window to the driveway was partly open, but I wondered if the fumes of oil paint and solvents might have been having an effect on his brain. I also wondered if, with all the chemicals filling the room, our furnace might explode.

"Don't stay up too late," I said. Dad didn't hear me, so

I popped my head farther into the room. "Not too late, okay, Dad?" I urged again.

"I never knew you had this bossy streak, Billy," Dad said. "You're making me feel like I'm the kid, not you." He rubbed a rag against a corner of the canvas. "How would you like to see a sample of the second stage of Bill Morrison's career?"

Dad grabbed the canvas's bottom edge with two hands and turned it toward me. He had painted a glorious, exuberant sunset, with piercing bright rays and layers of tinted clouds—but where you would expect to see orange, gold, red, and purple, Dad's painting was only gray and black. I didn't know much about art. I thought only that this painting was a big disappointment. Dad waited, but I didn't want to break his heart by saying what I felt.

"I'm glad you're having fun with this," I said, hoping he hadn't read my expression as I pulled the door closed.

15.

breakfast with champions

.

That was intense," Dad said, standing at the kitchen counter with a huge mug of black coffee. He hadn't showered or shaved, and he was still wearing yesterday's clothes.

From the kitchen, I looked out over the low brick divider and through the living room's picture window. A school bus picked up some first graders across the street. "How late were you up last night?" Mom asked. "I never heard you come into the bedroom."

"Oh, two or three," Dad said. He hummed "Barcarolle" and laughed to himself, as if his painting were a friend he had spent the night talking to.

"I hope you don't make this a habit," Mom said. "You're going to be useless at work today." She pulled aside the kitchen curtains and checked the traffic going by on the highway on the other side of our fence. "But it's good to see you so excited about something."

"Did you finish your painting?" Linda asked, squeezing

an orange on Grandma Pearl's old juicer. "When are you going to show it to us?"

"Not for a while," Dad said. "Billy got a preview, but I had so much fun, I think I'll squirrel away the paintings for now and show you all of them at once."

I thought again about the gray sunset. It was disturbing. What was Dad trying to get at? And why would he spend so much money on different paint colors if he wasn't going to use them?

I got up from the table and shook the box of oatmeal squares in his direction. "Bowl of cereal, Dad? How about eating something?"

"I'm fine with just the coffee." He hardly saw the Quaker guy on the box. It was overshadowed by the picture in his head.

"At least a Pop-Tart." I went to the cabinet for a smaller box. I didn't like this at all. Last winter began because Dad didn't eat or sleep. We couldn't get him into a normal routine again.

Dad chuckled. "Adele, how did we raise such a bossy child?" He shook his head, shrugged, and laughed again.

"Maybe he won't be a psychologist after all," Mom said. "Maybe he'll be the CEO of a Fortune 500 company." She started pulling together what she needed for the day: purse, laptop, cell phone, and a briefcase of magazines and papers.

"No, that's Linda," Dad said. Linda found ways to monetize everything. Most of her artwork evolved into a moneymaking scheme. She and Jodie had tried to sell clay cats, hand-pounded wrapping paper, and origami Mother's Day cards.

"You *are* going to work today, aren't you, Bill?" Mom looked a little worried.

"Afraid so," he said, "but I wish I could spend all day painting. I hate to break off what I love doing and spend eight hours on meaningless labor. Why aren't we rich? Why didn't I think of that, Adele? Why did you let me forget to become rich?"

"You'd better get in the shower," Mom said, putting her bag over her shoulder. "Linda, are you going to need a ride, or will you catch the bus?"

"Ride." Linda drank her juice with ice cubes and went to finish getting ready. Mom made a few calls in the living room while she waited.

"Dad. Pop-Tart." I unwrapped a strawberry pastry and put it on a paper plate in front of Dad. He nibbled at the corners. My gaze dropped to his abdomen under the paint-spattered T-shirt. Already that little potbelly was flattening out.

"I'm onto something big," Dad said.

"With your sunset?" I shook the plate so he would remember to eat.

"With my painting in general." He dropped his voice to a whisper. "And I shouldn't keep it all to myself."

"You're going to show Mom and Linda after all?" I rinsed my bowl for the dishwasher.

"That's not what I mean." Dad ran his hand over his rough, stubbly face. I wondered if he had been cold in just a T-shirt last night. It was early November, and I had heard the wind rattling. Was he even aware of his physical sensations when he painted?

"I mean, work like what I'm producing right now has to be seen. I'm going to start contacting museums and galleries and see if someone wants to give me a show, or at least represent me."

"That one painting? The gray one? Or are you talking about what you worked on in school?"

"The new stuff. I don't care as much about the old stuff. Okay, maybe the old stuff too. But these new paintings I'm going to be working on—someone will want to show them. I've got to reactivate my old contacts."

Dad had eaten only a quarter of the Pop-Tart. "You know what I'm going to say, right?" I asked. "Before I even say it?" I reached toward him, and he did the high-five. "How about just painting for fun and not worrying about the rest of it?"

"Because those of us who have special gifts are obligated to share them with others," he said, as if it were self-explanatory. He leaned closer and whispered again. "We carry the fire, Billy."

For a second I thought he meant "we" as in him and me. When I realized he probably didn't I snorted and didn't really care. I could take my family in stride today. Tonight I would have my first Listeners shift, manning the phones and saving actual callers from suicide.

"Bill Senior, you're still standing in the same spot! You've got to get moving!" Mom said as she kissed Dad and not me.

"Now she thinks she's my boss too." Dad laughed and rushed down the hall to take a shower.

shift 1, november 4

I clipped my Listeners photo ID to my shirt pocket and slid my passcard through the electronic reader outside the elevator. Pep had scheduled me on the five-to-nine shift Tuesdays and Fridays with Margaret and Richie. It would be a busy shift because the Incomings who worked all day or went to school would be getting home and ready to talk.

I arrived fifteen minutes early, as Pep requested, so I had some time to chill with my mates. I felt nervous—but a good, preshow, big-game nervous. Purposeful. I asked Margaret why she had joined Listeners.

Margaret, it turned out, started with Listeners six months ago. She joined because of her religious beliefs. She didn't believe in any kind of killing, including suicide, abortion, or capital punishment.

I asked her if she killed bugs, and she said she tried not to.

Richie said he wanted to save lives but he was not

entirely against suicide. Although Listeners said the most tragic thing about suicide was that it was a permanent solution to a temporary problem, Richie believed it was a legitimate choice in some circumstances, such as terminal illness. He said, in fact, that he would consider offing himself if he were terminally ill. I looked closely at Richie, with his new-for-school pencil case and his Ninja Turtles T-shirt. How would he do it—stage a head-on collision in his go-kart?

Margaret asked why I had joined. She called me Mr. Newcomer. I told her that, like some of the volunteers in the website video, I had a close family member who had been suicidal. As I told her this I placed my hand on the phone, and even though Dad's heart was in his artwork these days and not in our relationship, I said aloud that I dedicated my service at Listeners to my CFM.

Margaret announced that it was ten minutes to five, a transitional moment. She went to a cabinet in the corner of the room that was labeled with a brass plaque:

EMMA P. BRAUMANN

MEMORIAL SNACK CABINET

FOR THE BENEFIT OF THE LISTENERS

IN PERPETUITY FOREVER

ENJOY!

Richie told me this cabinet was restocked daily from an endless supply of snacks. The snacks came in handy, especially during the overnight shifts the college-age Listeners were required to man. The selection of food was not great—not microwave nachos or anything—but it was always there.

Margaret came back with a plastic bag.

Inside were circus peanuts, that strange food that is pale orange, resembles a bloated peanut, and tastes neither like peanuts nor like anything orange but like marshmallow.

Richie warned me not to get caught chewing when the phone rang.

I swallowed the pale orange wad, which no amount of saliva could effectively moisten.

Two minutes to five. Almost showtime. Richie folded his arms and stared at the phones, a very old-fashioned kind that you would think was too obsolete to work—beige plastic, the receiver attached to the base with a squiggly coil. I took a deep breath. Any Incomings would go automatically to Margaret, the veteran, on line 1. If her line was busy, the call would bounce to Richie on line 2. Manning line 3, I'd get the fewest calls.

Line 1 rang, and Margaret pressed the button.

Soon both Margaret and Richie were talking to Incomings. Their listening, though professional, had a different quality from what I'd witnessed with Dad's therapist, Dr. Fritz. Fritz was hugely into eye contact. Here, Margaret doodled. Richie arranged circus peanuts end to end. His voice seemed different on the phone: low, sincere, and commiserative, it might make Incomings believe he was my age. On a scrap of paper I wrote a song title: "Check In Before You Check Out." Then, holy cripes, my phone lit. Line 3 was ringing. Someone needed me. Someone was in trouble, and I was going to save them. Margaret and Richie dropped their listening faces and glanced at me with big, encouraging eyes. For a second I felt overwhelmed. I hesitated. Richie covered his mouthpiece with one hand and motioned at me to pick up.

I grabbed the receiver.

17.

call 1

Listeners. Can I help you?"
Yeah. How's it going?
"Not bad. How's it going with you?"
All right.
"What's happening?"
Not much. Have you seen Mineral Man?
"Why, is it good?"
So you haven't seen it?
"Have you seen it?"
I saw it last night! The special effects were incredible! There was a scene where Mineral Man turned an entire city into a white mineral—the buildings, the people, the cars, even the food—and it sparkled so much that even though it was nighttime it looked like the middle of the day.
"Sounds like you really enjoyed it. My name's Billy, by the way."
Do you read any comics?
"I don't know."
You don't know?

52

Oh, cripes. I wasn't supposed to reveal anything about myself, but what kind of idiot doesn't know whether he reads comics or not? Not very convincing. I had to get the hang of that.

"I mean, I've looked at them, sure, but I don't know much about them. Is Mineral Man your favorite?"

Well, some people are upset that the movie is a complete departure from the comic, but I think it completely adds to the comic. When I go to a movie I like to see the character be fairly complex, with both a dark side and a light side, you know? And in this one we get to see Seth's dark side in a way we've never seen it before. I really don't understand why anyone would be trashing it. And it's the same director who did Varga. *I think, in a way, it upsets the public for the director to do something different than he did before. To have a different style or whatever.*

"Yep."

Well, what do you think? Do you agree?

"It sounds like you have really strong feelings about movies."

It really ticks me off when people go to a movie just expecting to be entertained.

"You seem a little angry."

What? Not really. I guess I'm just intense. Or passionate. Passionate about movies.

"So you're not upset?"

No. I'm having fun with this. This is cool.

"Sorry to interrupt, but—are you feeling suicidal?"

It was awkward to bring this up out of nowhere. But kind of a thrill, too. What if he said yes?

No.

"Okay, we ask everyone that."

I know. And the answer is no.

"Do you want to tell me your first name?"

I'm Carl.

"Okay, Carl, do you want to get back to what you were saying?"

With a little probing, Carl outlined Books 1, 2, and 3 of the Mineral Man saga. I started to realize one of the benefits of open-ended questions: I could probe forever without making a statement that would reveal I had no idea what I was talking about. And Carl loved to explain, so it worked for us both.

Margaret tapped her watch. My booklet said to limit most calls to five minutes.

"I should go. But it's been great talking with you. Learning about . . . Seth and everyone."

My pleasure, dude.

18.

splashdown

I waited for Margaret and Richie to finish their calls. Margaret put her line on hold and told Richie and me to do the same. Then she touched my shoulder and asked if I was okay.

Richie bumped my fist and said I was initiated. He asked how I liked my call from the Carl Planet. It had been awkward, I told him, because I was never into comics the way Carl was. And the call hadn't been what I expected, because Carl wasn't upset or suicidal. He wasn't even slightly sad.

Richie said the important thing was that I had listened.

I told them the video had made me think everyone who called would be suicidal.

Hold on there, Margaret cautioned me. She said newbies often came in thinking they were Superman, but they rarely got to save anyone the first night. Or even the first month. Some people got a Likely the first day, she explained, and others worked at Listeners for years without a single Likely.

Margaret was right, Richie added. We couldn't come in to work and only value the Likelies. We had to think of each Incoming as equally important, even if they called just to talk about the weather.

I asked him why, if an Incoming wanted to talk about the weather, he or she called us and not someone else.

Maybe there was no one else, Richie said. Maybe they were lonely and isolated.

Or maybe they were tired of putting up a front for other people, Margaret suggested. Maybe Listeners was the only place these Incomings could be themselves.

I said nothing for a minute. I was beginning to feel like I had made a bad decision. Should I have started a band with Gordy after all?

Keep plugging, my ListMates told me. I would get a feel for it after a while. I should keep listening, they said. If not for the callers, then for my CFM. I thought of Dad then. Dad was at home, painting industriously, having the time of his life. How had it worked out that he was happy with what he was doing and I wasn't?

Margaret opened her line and we started again.

call 2

Listeners. Can I help you?"

How old are you?

"I'm sorry, but I can't give out personal information. Anyway, I'd rather hear what's going on with you."

You're just a kid, aren't you?

A man's voice—smooth, like a radio announcer.

"How are things going?"

You sound really young.

"My name's Billy. Would you like to tell me your first name?"

Are you wearing boxers or briefs?

My hand went instinctively to my thigh. "I'm sorry?"

Right now. Do you have on boxers or briefs?

"Do I . . . ?"

You know what I'm talking about.

"I have to go." *Click.*

20.

lowered expectations

I continued for a few more calls. The handbook said I should get people to discuss their feelings, but two Incomings refused to name a single feeling, and I wasn't sure they even had any. One said his major feeling was discomfort because he had never talked to me before. Another asked if she could talk to Margaret or Richie instead. When I finished that call, I looked at the clock. Eight forty-five. My phone rang.

call 12

"Listeners. Can I help you?"

Yep. It's Jenney. I had a really tough day today.

"I'm sorry to hear that."

I walked past Hawthorne State and I started thinking about all that stuff again, about everything I'm missing.

"Everything you're missing?"

Yeah, the fact that I'm supposed to be in school now and I'm not. I just can't face school in the condition I'm in. But I saw all these Staties on their way to a game or a rally or something, and they have big groups of friends and lots of ways to fill their time. They have everything I was supposed to have, everything I was going to have, but . . . My future got taken away from me.

I heard a soft clicking sound, like the feet of a cat on a hardwood floor.

"Jenney, are you crying?"

Yes . . . I'm sorry . . . I'm such a mess. Just give me a sec to pull myself together.

"Take your time. Don't worry about crying. That's what we're here for."

Okay. A little better now.

"Jenney, are you thinking about suicide?"

Oh, God—no. You don't have to ask me that. Suicide is for weaklings. I'm a fighter, you know.

"That's great. You sound like a really strong person."

I really am strong, I think. I would have to be strong to go through what I'm going through.

"You should be proud of that, Jenney."

I am.

"So, do you want to tell me what's going on? What happened with school? You seem disappointed about the school situation."

Because of all the stuff that happened with my parents, I didn't—

"I'm sorry, what happened with your parents?"

You don't know?

"No, I don't."

You must know. Everybody at Listeners knows what happened with my parents.

"Well, I don't. I'm sorry to interrupt you, because you're obviously upset, but I'd like to get more background if you want to tell me."

Wait a minute . . . are you new?

"Yes, I am. This is my first day, actually. My name is Billy, by the way."

I can't believe it. You're great *at this!*

"I am?"

*Yeah, I would never have thought this was your first day.
I feel so comfortable talking to you.*

"Really?"

I feel like I could tell you anything.

"Well, thanks."

Margaret cleared her throat. I realized I was breaking one of the rules.

"It's great of you to say so, but I'm not here to talk about myself. I'd much rather hear about you and school and everything." Margaret nodded. She returned to her doodles and her Incoming.

All right. Well. Jenney took a deep breath. *I've been through some changes lately. A lot of changes, and not for the better. Hello? Are you there?*

"Yes. Go ahead."

Okay, I was all set to start college, at St. Angus's. Do you know St. Angus's?

"Tell me about it."

It's an elite women's college in New Hampshire. It's often called the Eighth Seven Sister.

"Mm-hmm."

My mother went there, and my grandmother and her mother, and so on from way, way back. It's really selective, and the women who graduate from there often become very successful. My mom made friends there that she's stayed in touch with for, like, her whole life. It's in Molton, one of those perfect little New England towns with the white church steeple in the center.

"It sounds great. What happened?"

Well, I got accepted. I mean, they were really excited about having me come to the school. The admissions office was.

Because not only would I probably have gotten in as a legacy because of my mom and grandmom and everybody, but I got in on my own merits. I think that's really important, don't you?

"You got in on your own merits."

You're repeating me. Don't you think that's important?

"It's important to you. That's what matters. So you got accepted."

Right. They offered me a partial scholarship because of my swimming.

"You're a swimmer."

Yes, I have a trophy and everything. Did you go to Hawthorne High?

"You have a trophy."

I have a trophy in Hawthorne High, in the case in the front lobby. Because my grades were great too. I can say that to you because you seem pretty smart yourself, and you won't think I'm conceited. So I actually got in to all three of my top schools that I applied to.

"And you decided to go somewhere else?"

I didn't go at all.

"Why not?"

Because I started freaking out. The summer before school. I had a kind of . . . breakdown. Like a meltdown.

"That sounds awful. I'm so sorry."

Well, it was awful. It was terrible. . . . It was a nightmare. The soft clicking sound started again, a shutter moving in the back of her throat.

"Take your time." I didn't know what else to say.

Okay. Jenney's voice was clear again. *It was late July, early August. I was getting ready for school—e-mailing my new roommate, buying odds and ends for the dorm room—and I suddenly felt like I was somewhere else. I got disoriented, and I panicked, like something really bad was about to happen. I didn't feel like Ms. Successful College Student. I felt small and helpless, like I was suffocating, and I could barely see the four walls around me, which were in my bedroom at home.*

"You felt small and helpless. Why do you think you felt that way?"

Because I was having a flashback. To my childhood. I was horribly abused as a child.

"By who?"

By my parents. Both of them.

"Your mother, too? Your mother who went to St. Angus's?"

That's right. My mother who went to St. Angus's. Who did everything right and was a big success story and a famous social butterfly. My mom who wrote books and my dad who owned a TV station. But the two of them, nobody knew it at the time, but those two were hurting me all along. These two supposedly great parents turned out to be the most evil people on the planet.

I looked at the clock—8:52. I had to end the call, but I had no idea how. What would I say? What Jenney's parents did was wrong. No parent had the right to hurt a kid. People like that shouldn't even have kids. That's what I would have said to someone else. But that was my opinion, and we didn't give opinions at Listeners.

"I'm so sorry, but I have to go in a minute."

I know you have to go. You have to go just when I pulled

off this scab that covers my heart. That's what they all say at Listeners.

"I can give you one more minute," I said. "I've really enjoyed talking to you. I hope things get better and I hope you call again."

All right, she said as the clicking began again. *That's the thing about Listeners. You expect us to turn our emotions off and on like a faucet.* I waited, and the clicking stopped. *All right, that's enough for tonight. I'm sure I'll be okay. You know, talking to you about all this made me feel a little better.*

"It did? I'm glad. I'm really glad you called, Jenney. I mean, we're really glad you called."

I do feel better. Talking to someone who believes me. You're a great guy, Billy, did you know that?

"Thanks. Good night, Jenney."

I can't believe you're new. You're practically the best one over there. 'Night.

22.

a dark side

Dial tone. Now I knew what Richie meant about the planets, because Jenney's world disappeared and I was back in the office. My replacement, a college student named Vince who would be covering the overnight shift, grasped the back of my chair.

I told him I was a little freaked out and needed a minute. I ran one hand over my hair and face. My skin felt damp. I wasn't sure what Jenney meant when she said she'd been abused. My parents had never hit me or Linda. I knew that kids got sexually abused, but I never knew anyone who said they did. And a kid in my neighborhood who moved from place to place often because his parents were in the military had a black eye a few times and his arm in a cast. My mom was disgusted and wanted to say something to his parents, but they moved away before she could say anything. What kind of hurting was Jenney talking about?

picturing

At the end of the shift, Margaret, Richie, and I took the elevator to the first floor of Cabot Insurance. Their parents picked them up while I unlocked my bike.

I found myself conjuring a face to match Jenney's voice. What would she look like? She was a swimmer and her parents were rich, so she was probably at least average. Athletes usually look good. And rich people can fix all the defects that poor people live with. She wouldn't have weird teeth or an odd-looking nose. A picture swam into my mind: a slim girl in a one-piece Olympic-style bathing suit, with wavy wheat-colored hair in a damp braid. But then I told myself that as a Listener I talked only to the inner person, so Jenney's looks didn't matter.

In high school everyone says how cool it is to be different or unusual, but most of your friendships are based on being alike, and the people who are most like everyone else seem to get the most friends. You can pick them out on sight, Generic High School Kid, because they're always either laughing or on the phone or both, and the fact that they're never left with their own thoughts makes everyone want to be their friend.

I was never that guy, and if Jenney had ever been that girl, she wasn't anymore.

2 4 .

beacon

My school is famous, or at least freakish, for having the only regulation football field in the United States that's below sea level. A deep canal was cut along the outer edge of the field, so we students get used to looking up from an English essay and seeing a sail appearing to coast through the grass, or a group of tourists lining the rail of a whale-watch boat and looking into the classroom with their binoculars. The clock tower above the administration building is a landmark for sailors and appears on many navigational charts, and all our sports teams are called Schooners.

The Monday after my first talk with Jenney, I locked my bike in front of the main doors and kept my eyes straight ahead as I passed the trophy cases. Just as Jenney's looks were none of my business, her last name and year of graduation were not my business either. Signs leading from the cases to the athletic department exhorted SUC-CESS DOESN'T COME TO YOU—YOU GO TO IT and BE LIKE A

POSTAGE STAMP: STICK TO ONE THING UNTIL YOU GET THERE.

In history of music, Mr. Gabler assigned us a five-page paper on the instrument of our choice. "That's five pages, five sources," he said. "The sources can be any type you want—blogs, TV shows, documentaries, YouTube videos, recordings—as long as you document them properly. For our next class I want you to give me your choice of instrument and your five sources."

Gordy walked to lunch with me after class. "How was it?" he asked.

"Kind of a letdown," I said. I looked at him for commiseration. "Nobody was actually suicidal."

"That's good, though, isn't it?" He stopped walking and watched my face. I could see he wanted to strike the correct tone but was confused.

"No, you're right. I'm glad no one was considering offing himself. But you know my neighbor who became an EMT? How he was all, like, puffed up when he got a medic certificate and came home in that uniform? I expected to feel like that. To get an adrenaline rush from saving lives."

Gordon stopped at his locker for his insulated lunch bag, and I wondered what was in it. A crowd of students came toward us. Andy walked behind a girl and imitated the sway of her butt, in an effort to make Mitchell laugh.

"Do me a favor, okay?" I asked Gordy, turning my back on the oncoming crowd.

"What's that?"

"Let's not tell the other guys what I just told you. I couldn't stand to have them rag on me again."

changing course

Dad ripped off his necktie as soon as he parked the car. Then he came inside and changed into his painting clothes.

"Nothing," he said as he cut through the house toward his studio. "Not one word."

"What's wrong?" Linda asked, following him into the kitchen. She wore a geriatric golf shirt and skirt. Jodie trailed behind, a purple plastic barrette hanging on a lank piece of hair in front of her eyes. As she trotted along, she swatted it back against the freckles on her cheek.

"I want my paintings to be seen, but no one's giving me encouragement. I wrote to the Institute of Contemporary Art, the Peabody Essex, the Cape Ann, the galleries in the South End and on Newbury Street, and the Rocky Neck artist-in-residence program. I even e-mailed some of my old classmates who have gallery connections. No one invited me to submit work. Sure, I can fill out applications and send slides. But mostly the galleries already know which artists they want, and go after them. And I don't have time to wait around."

"People are stupid, aren't they, Mr. Morrison?" Jodie asked.

"Not stupid, exactly," Dad said. He chewed on his lip before speaking again. "They just can't recognize something good if it's not like a hundred things they haven't seen before."

"That's really frustrating, Mr. Morrison," Jodie said.

Mom was flipping through the mail and checking the answering machine. "Oh well, honey," she said. "If you're going to keep pushing the envelope, you have to expect a paper cut."

"Cute," Dad said. He folded his arms over his chest. He looked furled, like an umbrella.

I had just started researching the history of the Hohner Special 20 harmonica. I dropped my work and went into the studio, where Dad's finished and half-finished paintings were turned toward the wall. I hoped I could say something to make him relax. To unfurl him.

"I'm doing my homework," I said. "I just want you to know that."

"I'm glad," he said. He didn't look glad. He pressed a fist into his mouth and chewed his lip harder.

I stretched up and rested a hand on the molding above the doorway. "Answer a question for me," I said. "Are you having a good time with your painting?"

"Up till now I was. Until the world conspired to teach me that art is unnecessary."

"See what's happening? One little disappointment and

you're not enjoying it anymore. That's what I was worried about. I wish you would be happy that you have something you enjoy doing and not worry about status and recognition. Live in the moment. No success, no failure." I let go of the molding and sort of fell into his room, but gracefully, like a trapeze artist.

"That's not good enough, though," Dad said. "I want more. I always thought . . ."

"Yes?" I asked, using my Listeners techniques.

Dad's body softened. With one hand he picked through the brushes on the table, lifting and dropping them like they were so much kindling.

"I thought I was going to have a *big* life. Be different from other people. You and Linda and your mom are great, but—"

I balked at this, but I talked myself through it: *It's not up to you to judge. You're living on the Dad Planet now.*

"You wanted to be different," I echoed.

Dad nodded to himself. He had made some kind of decision. "I'm going to have the big life," he said. "I'll make the opportunities for myself if no one will make them for me."

26.

last winter: red all over

Dad's first antidepressant has given him what Dad's psychiatrist, Dr. Gupta, calls an "atypical dermatological reaction." That means that Dad is covered with blisters—red lumps that merge to make ridges, with yellow pus forming streams in between. Some of the blisters look like numbers or letters: D or 8. He keeps discovering more, and Linda and I pantomime gagging every time his back is turned. Mom tells him not to look at his skin and to keep his sleeves rolled down. Soon the rash disturbs him more than anything else that is wrong. We cover up all the mirrors.

shift 2, november 8

Margaret and Richie were both on calls. Margaret smiled and nodded even though the Incoming couldn't see her. Funny how the visual signals humans developed face-to-face persisted when we were separated.

She asked her caller something about a fiancé in Iraq. A gold cross sparkled against Margaret's plaid uniform. She zinged the cross from side to side on its chain while she talked. Mom often did something like that too. She touched her necklace when she was nervous, as if it held magical powers. Richie's arm partly blocked my view and my hearing, but I heard him say "amputation" and "prosthesis." I had to give him props: He could handle more than I thought.

I waited in pregame mode, thinking about that last conversation with Dad. What had he been trying to tell me?

I thought I was going to have a big life. Be different from other people. You and Linda and your mom are great, but—

What would he have said if I hadn't interrupted him?

I'm going to have the big life. I'll make the opportunities.

Maybe he'd been about to ask for my help: *I'll make the opportunities. And I want the three of you to be part of it.* Or maybe he was saying we were in his way. Maybe he was saying he was going to leave us.

I knew what he meant by a "big life." He and Mom and Linda and even Jodie were great, but they weren't enough for me, either. When I became a psychologist, I wanted a big life too.

Line 3 rang, and I rested my hand on the receiver for a second before answering. The heck with my CFM. I wasn't doing this for him. I was doing it for me.

call 1

"Listeners. Can I help you?"

I don't feel safe.

"Why are you not feeling safe, ma'am?"

You better whisper. They'll hear us.

"Who'll hear us?"

The CIA.

"The CIA is bugging your phone?"

Richie glanced over and nodded. He'd had this Incoming before.

No, my bathtub.

"That sounds really upsetting. My name is Billy. Would you like to tell me your first name?"

Debra. Last week I couldn't take a bath because they were in there.

"And you say this started a week ago?"

Approximately.

"How did they get in?"

Through the water pipes.

"You sound pretty calm about what's going on."

Oh, well. That's life. Can't fight City Hall, right?

"You're a very brave person, Debra." I stretched the cord and twirled it around my finger.

What else can I do? I have to live with it.

"Do you have any idea why the CIA would do this to you?"

Am I being recorded?

"Absolutely not. This line is confidential."

I'll tell you, then: Because my parents were spies.

"How did you find out?"

When they died I found a book about Cuba. Something inside the cover was erased.

"That must have been a shock."

No one knows but the CIA. I barely talk to my neighbors.

"It must be hard to trust people when you have a secret like that."

I asked Debra, since she rarely left the house, if she was buying food, if she was eating okay. I tried to focus on Debra's well-being. It wasn't my job to separate fact from fiction. I could let go and surf on the untruth of everything she said.

calls 2-4

After Debra, I got two nearly identical calls from teenagers who had been dumped, and one from an elderly man who seemed to be drunk.

It's my birthday, he kept saying.

"Happy birthday," I said three times.

He asked me to sing, but I didn't. With hardly a bobble, I made all three Incomings feel a little better. None was suicidal.

call 12

"Listeners. Can I help you?"

It's me. I'm having a really bad night.

Jenney. I remembered her, but I couldn't say so.

"I'm sorry to hear that. Do you want to tell me your first name?"

You don't know who I am?

"No, I don't. My name's Billy. Would you like to tell me your name?"

It's Jenney. Don't you remember? We talked a few nights ago.

"I'm sorry," I said again.

It's okay, Billy. I know you have to do that.

"You said you're having a bad night. What's going on?"

I just came from a really rough session with Melinda.

"Melinda?" Start from scratch. Clean slate. Every time.

My therapist. She's helping me to go back into my childhood and dig stuff up.

"Are you feeling suicidal?"

No.

"How does your therapist dig this stuff up? And what kind of stuff do you mean?"

One night, during the summer I graduated from high school, I woke up to this feeling of something pressing into my neck. It seemed so real, as if it were actually happening. But I woke up and I saw that I was alone in my room as usual. I'm an only child, see—I didn't share my room with anyone. Then I walked down the hall and stuck my head in the door of my parents' room, and they were both sound asleep. No one had broken into the house; no one had touched me. So, though it felt real, I figured it was just a nightmare.

"That seems really upsetting. What was that feeling?"

It started to happen more often—waking up at night with the distinct feeling that something was pressing around my neck. I came to expect it, that I would wake up every night in a panic and not be able to get back to sleep. I wasn't sleeping all that well. Maybe three hours a night.

"You must have been exhausted."

Yeah, I was. The tiredness didn't hit me all at once, but after a week or so it started taking a toll on me. And I didn't feel like staying out late anymore, and my friends stopped calling me. You assume that people like you for yourself, but then something changes and you see that they only liked you for some other reason. Like that you have a car and can drive them around. Or what you look like. Or who your parents are. You know?

"Uh-huh." No one had ever liked me for those reasons. But I could relate.

I'm supposed to be in school right now, you know, a really good school. I already told you that last time, but you probably don't remember.

I remembered. That really good selective school in New Hampshire. "Do you want to be in school?"

Yes and no. Anyway, I tried to drag myself along at that level, living day to day, but I had this weird feeling, like dread, that was building up inside me, and on one of the rare occasions when I discussed anything important with my mom she sent me to a counselor who specialized in anxiety disorders. That doctor, who I saw only once, said it looked like I needed to see someone who deals with repressed memories. And that was how I found Melinda.

"Did she help you?"

She changed my whole life. The first time I went into her office she asked if there was any possibility that I'd been abused as a kid and didn't remember. I got really quiet—it was like time was standing still—and then I felt this huge sadness come up from somewhere inside me that I hadn't even known was there, and I couldn't talk for about ten minutes . . . and then Melinda said, not in an accusing way, but in a kind of gentle, all-accepting way, because she's a very gentle person, she said, "Why are you protecting them, Jenney?"

Margaret and Richie whispered about her last call, but I was barely aware of them. "'Why are you protecting them?'" I asked Jenney. "Meaning who?"

Meaning my parents.

The parents were abusive. "She meant that your parents had hurt you in some way. Had abused you."

Exactly.

Mirror. Reflect. "I'm so sorry, Jenney. It must have been really awful to find that out."

Believe me, it was. My parents were having a dinner that night for two couples they had known since college, and I almost didn't want to go home. After I left Melinda's I called my parents and made an excuse about needing to go to the library, and I didn't go home until after nine when the library closed, and I shut myself in my room and shut out the laughter and the dishes clinking and the music and everything else from the dinner party, and I just emptied myself out and allowed myself to feel nothing, just the way I did at Melinda's. Because it was easier to feel nothing than to feel the pain of what had really happened, the pain of the betrayal. And then something else happened.

"What was that?"

After the whole neck thing, I started getting another feeling that seemed real. On my face. The feeling of something cold and hard on my cheek. Like stone. And I worked really hard in my sessions with Melinda. She regressed me and took me back through all the years and all the pain—oh, God, I nearly turned myself inside out—and we figured out what it meant.

"The feeling on your face? What was it?"

Melinda kept saying, "Where are you, Jenney? Where are you when your face feels so cold?" It was the floor of the basement of our house. We figured out that when I misbehaved my parents would take me to the basement and choke me with a cord until I passed out. And that my body had never forgotten that feeling. The pressure of the cord around my neck and the coldness of the floor under my face. And then she said it again: "Why are you protecting them, Jenney?"

"Why were you protecting them?"

Jenney's clicking started again. My own throat tightened when I heard it.

Because I was a child, and every child needs her parents.

Get her to pull back. To look at the big picture.

"With everything you have going on, Jenney, what do you think bothers you most about your situation?"

Not being in school. Seeing other kids at school and knowing that's supposed to be me. Knowing that I'm not moving forward in my life. It bothered my mom, too, maybe even more. When I started having my meltdown, she hardly cared about me as a person. She would watch me sleeping too much and eating too much and coming out of my room with my eyes red from crying and she would say, "What's going to happen with St. Angus's?" The two of them—all they care about is status.

But Melinda says I need to delay college for a while and keep working on the abuse. Yes, I should be in school, but that has to wait until I get myself straightened out. I mean, what kind of shape am I in to be starting anything new? How could I study? How could I concentrate? How could I meet people?

"I don't think you would have any trouble making friends." Find traits to compliment.

My friends don't want to be around me anymore. I invited my two friends to the movies and they said they were busy. That's what I really miss, you know?

"What do you miss?" Exact words.

Being normal. Having a normal day or a normal night. Going to the movies with my friends. Walking across the parking lot. You know how you feel on a weekend night, like everybody's more alive, like everybody's looking at you. Like people expect something exciting or funny or unusual to happen, even if you're just in the mall. Deciding what to get for snacks—pizza or Dibs? And then forgetting everything and watching a whole movie beginning to end, munching my snack, without having an attack or a flashback. . . . It would be, like, There's a whole world out here, you know? Are you still there?

"A whole world."

Yeah. Jenney got quiet for a moment.

Melinda says to put everything on hold. She says getting to the bottom of my memories has to be my number one priority in life.

Jenney had said she repressed the memories because they were too painful. While she spoke, I tried imagining what it would be like to be afraid of your own memories. I had bad memories too, of last winter and other times, but I didn't have trouble remembering them, because they were not as bad as Jenney's. They were tolerable. I tried to imagine memories that lurked at the edge of other memories, ready to pounce like something from a horror movie.

"You must be very strong to get through something like this. Did you ever confront your parents?"

Of course.

"And what did they say?"

They said none of it was true. They said I was making it up. And then they blamed Melinda for ruining our relationship. Of course they're not going to admit it.

I felt Margaret's touch on my arm. It got more insistent, a strong pinch on my elbow. She had leaned across Richie's station to signal me. I kept my cell phone on the table to time my calls. Six minutes had gone by, but Jenney seemed so upset that I couldn't hang up now.

Have you ever been through a crisis?

"Well . . ."

You have. I can tell. Maybe you can talk about it sometime. And it'll be my turn to listen.

"I hope you get your movie soon. It sounds like it'll be fun."

I hope so too.

"I have to go."

You helped me a lot, you know, just by being there.

"I'm really happy you called. And I hope you keep feeling better today. And the day after that, and the day after that." When I heard a smile in her voice, I would know it was time to stop.

You sound like a greeting card.

"I really meant it."

Maybe I'll call you Hallmark.

Margaret tapped me and pointed to the wall clock.

You're actually cheering me up, you know that? I just laughed for the first time in a long time.

"I'm glad I could help. I've got to go now, Jenney. It's been really good talking to you."

Okay, but . . . Billy, I'm sorry for what I said.

"Meaning what?"

That you were a greeting card.

"That's okay."

If you are a Hallmark card, you're one of the expensive ones. On the upper shelves. Four dollars.

"I'd like to think that's true. I'm sorry you're feeling down. Better days ahead, I hope."

Maybe. Bye, Billy.

burgers and fries

Margaret and Richie put their phones on hold.

Margaret asked if that had been Jenney on the phone. I told her it was.

Jenney was a sweet person who got sort of down sometimes, Margaret said. But it wasn't our job to entertain Jenney or cheer her up. The Incomings would make themselves feel better, she told me, if I let them take the lead.

I understood, I said, but I had to tell them something else. Something emotional.

Richie encouraged me to spill.

I said I felt bad that I couldn't let on I remembered Jenney. I knew her feelings were hurt. And she had been through so much. I loved that I could put a smile on her face.

Richie thought that Jenney was playing me a little.

Jenney was pleasant and even fun, Margaret said. That was why I remembered our conversation. But what if I got someone who wasn't fun? Or what if I remembered part of Jenney's story but not all? Someone's feelings were bound to be hurt. Better to appear to remember nothing.

Besides, Richie said, the program only worked when it was consistent. The Incoming had to have the same experience whether she got me, Richie, or Margaret.

I reached for the hold button. I would be consistent, I announced. Like fast-food burgers.

Richie bumped my fist. He joked that next week we'd install the drive-through window.

32.

self-evaluation

At the end of my shift I popped into the front room to say good night to Pep. I was starting to get comfortable on the phones, I told her. I sat on the edge of her table while she kept the phone on hold.

Pep agreed. She had lurked in the doorway once or twice and thought I sounded good. But I had to limit myself to five minutes per call. Each phone had a device that counted how many calls we took, and Richie and Margaret each handled about twice my volume.

Didn't the booklet say we could make a judgment call in some cases and allow ten? Only if it was a true cry for help, Pep said. If the Incoming was just de-stressing from the day or wanted company, I could accomplish plenty in five.

Pep squeezed my forearm and said good night. She probably meant to be encouraging, but the fact that she felt free to touch me accentuated the difference in our ages and reminded me again of June Melman.

I looked at the poster of an undercaffeinated man staring out the window. He seemed to be wondering when he would get a more visible modeling job.

I asked Pep if she had really ever gotten a Likely. She said she had had several. But how did she know whether they lived or died, I asked.

Pep stepped away from the table so the Incomings wouldn't hear us. If the Likelies called back on another day, she said, they were still alive. And if they didn't call back . . . Her upper body straightened like a coat going over a coathanger. If they were local, she explained, we might see something in the newspaper and put two and two together. Suicide was rarely listed as the cause of death. A family would rather say just that the deceased died suddenly than that he killed himself. And if an Incoming was from out of state, as they occasionally were, we would probably never know what happened.

Pep told me to head home. She hit her hold button and went back to womanning the phones.

plan to fail

It was good for someone like me to have someone like Mr. Gabler around. I was not chic or stylish, but Mr. Gabler was even less so. His clothes were thin and cheap-looking, and he was the last balding middle-aged man in America to comb his remaining hair in a long arc from ear to ear rather than shaving his head. When people made fun of him, I had the luxury of making fun too.

Despite his timid appearance, Gabler had taught music in prisons, and the classroom displayed posters of his single-sex productions of *Chicago, The Best Little Whorehouse in Texas,* and *The Threepenny Opera.*

Today he walked from desk to desk collecting the first phase of our music history paper. People seemed psyched as they handed in their ideas. Gordy had selected the Dobro, a guitar with a built-in resonater that functioned as an amp. Part of his research would be an e-mail interview with B. B. King. Nathan Brandifield was researching the theremin, an eerie-sounding electronic instrument that's played without being touched. Brenda Mason would write about handbells, since she played in her church bell choir.

"Oh, man," I said, holding my notebook in front of my face. I had meant to do this last night, but I did my shift at Listeners and then fell asleep on the couch.

I saw fingertips pry my notebook away, and Mr. Gabler appeared in front of my desk.

"Forget something?" he asked.

"I don't have my phase-one ideas. I'm sorry, Mr. Gabler."

"Can you e-mail them to me at the end of class?"

"I don't have them at all. It completely slipped my mind."

"What instrument are you writing about?"

"The harmonica."

"What sources?"

"The Hohner website, the Smithsonian CD series, a music encyclopedia, the guy at the music store, and an old recording on YouTube," Gordy suggested.

"That's right," I said. I wrote them on a piece of paper and tore it out for Mr. Gabler.

"No handwritten assignments," he said, laying the paper on my desk. "Get some specifics down and make sure you have your paper finished next Friday with everyone else." He propped my notebook up again to block my face.

"School success is so random," I said to Gordon on the way to lunch. We had passed a poster saying IF YOU FAIL TO PLAN, YOU PLAN TO FAIL. "What difference does it make in the long run? It seems more about generating status for your parents than about genuinely helping you create a happy future." I was thinking about Jenney, how her mother had only seemed to care whether Jenney moved like a robot through the stages laid out for her.

"It doesn't help at all to look at school that way," Gordon said, stopping inside the door of the cafeteria.

"Then how should I look at it?" I shifted my books from one side to the other.

Gordon lowered his voice so a group of Generic Laughing Guys headed to the food line wouldn't hear. "You're smart, right? So am I. So how hard is it to do the work they're asking for? This stuff is easy. Just finish it and save the rest of your brain for something else."

"But all the time they're asking us to put into it," I argued. "What if you spent your time on stuff like school assignments and in the meantime life—real life—was passing you by? How do we know that our real life, the big life we were meant to have, isn't now rather than in the future? What if nobody realized that about you? And what if you never got a chance at a big life again?"

Mitchell had sneaked up behind me. He stuck his face between mine and Gordon's. "They stick us here to isolate us from the rest of society," he whispered. "Because they're afraid of us. And no matter what they say, there is no other reason." He nodded at Gordon and me like he had figured out a big conspiracy, then he slid along the wall like he was escaping from someone. I couldn't help thinking about CIA Debra and the people she thought were after her.

Actually, I was glad to be stuck at school for so many hours of the week. The only places I wanted to be were at school, on my bike, or, preferably, at Listeners. I didn't like being at home anymore, since Dad started painting again. I felt like he didn't even want me there.

PART 2

crock or van gogh?

Each day, Dad became more inspired. He went to the town dump and scavenged wooden panels that had been ripped out of shelves or bookcases. He got worked up over political issues he had never mentioned before, particularly immigration law, the Federal Reserve Bank, gay rights, and drilling for oil in the Arctic wildlife refuge. Strangest of all, he was working on a group of paintings that looked just . . .

There was only one word for them: bizarre. At least two of them showed sad, bodiless heads, with faces of different colors, arranged in fruit bowls. Another was an orange largemouth bass jumping over a rainbow in which the colors were only black, white, and gray. I hoped he wasn't planning to show them to anyone.

Without indicating that I supported or liked Dad's work, I found an excuse to check on him every day. This time I found him not in his studio but in the conversation area, where he cursed over his notebook computer and deleted e-mails one after the other. Linda was lying on the other couch with her feet over the end, reading a dystopian novel.

"I've officially sent photos to twenty galleries and museums," Dad said. "And I haven't heard a word back from anybody." I cringed when I heard this. I hated the idea of Dad making a fool of himself. I pictured someone at the Peabody Essex Museum pulling up a JPEG of the fish painting and getting everybody in the office to gawk at it. Dad's activities could be especially harmful to Mom, because she worked in a museum and was supposed to know better. "I'm no longer waiting for life to act on me. I have to act on life."

"Meaning?" I asked.

"I'm giving myself a show."

"*Wow*," Linda said, sitting up and moving closer to Dad. "Where? Here?"

"In the garage. On December fourth."

"*This* December fourth?" I asked.

"I want to make the most of my time on this earth. Not sit around taking up space and valuable oxygen. I feel a need to justify my existence, you know?"

I felt like a hand had slipped between my ribs. It reached into my chest and started squeezing my heart. "What would be involved? It sounds like a huge deal."

"The biggest part is getting my work done—making the paintings. But I'll also have to get the garage ready, frame the paintings, display each piece, and—last but maybe most important—get the word out. Get the right people to show up." His legs stretched out on the ottoman, and his feet moved like puppets while he talked.

"I don't think this is a good move, Dad," I told him.

"Why not?"

"You're not allowing enough time," I said. "If you want to do a big project like this, why don't you wait till next summer and have everything just the way you want it?" I sat on the edge of the ottoman, next to Dad's feet. I wished I could grab them and do something funny with his toes that would lighten up my message. Mom and Linda both communicated with Dad in playful ways. Guys couldn't do that, other than punching.

"That will be part of it. The race to finish will be part of the process. The name of my show will be *Bill Morrison: Forty Paintings in Forty Days.*"

"That's a good gimmick," Linda said. "It almost sounds like a reality show."

"That's right. I hope curiosity will bring people in. Maybe I could get national media attention."

"Whoa," I said. "No one can paint forty paintings in forty days."

"Van Gogh did it. At the end of his life he painted seventy paintings in seventy days."

"Then what happened?"

"He shot himself."

"You're kidding."

"No, I'm serious."

How could Dad even joke about that? Did he think that because I was with Listeners I took a casual view of any mention of suicide? Or that because he was recovered, joking about it was okay?

"I assume you'll help me. You two, Mom, and Jodie. Am I wrong?"

"We'd love to help," Linda said. She jumped up from the couch, already halfway to calling Jodie. "Just tell me what you need us to do."

Dad leaned forward the way a football coach might in the locker room before a big game (not that I've ever seen this). "You two can be my apprentices. I'll outsource some of the basics to you so I can save myself for the creative work. And you'll learn enough in the process that someday you can turn seriously to painting too."

I stood in front of Dad with my hands in my pockets. I realized that I liked taking stands. I felt as definitive now as I had when I signed the Listeners confidentiality contract. *No exceptions, ever, period.* "I will not be helping, because I don't support this."

Dad shook his head. "Is this what passes in your world as your rebellious adolescent stage?"

"Look. I don't want you to get worn out. You should have a normal routine. No stress, no worries, no late nights."

But there was more: more stuff I would never say to Dad. I told him only the edge of what I was thinking, the acceptable edge. I hoped he knew the rest without my saying it. I hoped he knew how scary it had been for us to watch him get sick.

And to watch him get treated. But no way could I say that to Dad. I could only hint around.

last winter: night terrors

Someone in the house screams. They're being murdered.

It's Dad. Someone is murdering Dad.

I run into his room with my bicycle pump. I will clobber the person killing Dad. If they start to kill me, too, I'll use my last ounce of strength to save my favorite parent. Dad cannot die this year. Dad must live.

My room is dark, but the lights are on where Dad is. Mom kneels beside the bed, pulling on his shoulder. "Stop screaming, Bill! Stop!"

I drop the tire pump. "Dad, what's wrong? Mom, what is he screaming for?"

"He's having a nightmare and I can't wake him up. Oh, God, if he doesn't calm down, he's going to give himself a heart attack." Mom looks scared. I've rarely seen a scared Mom or heard a screaming Dad. Aaaaa*aah*, *aaa*aaaah! The sound climbs from low to high, then drops down and starts again, the way an opera singer would warm up his or her voice, if he or she were also terrified. It doesn't sound like when he's angry or when he sings. It's Dad's voice in a freakish, distorted mirror.

I climb on the bed beside him, holding his other shoulder, whispering fast, like someone praying in a foreign language—*Dadpleasewakeup, you'rescaringMom, you'rescaringmetoo,pleasewakeupandbenormalagain, pleasebewellagain.*

"That's it," Mom says, trying to look calm. "I'm calling 911."

"Aaaaa*aah, aaa*aaaah!"

Linda peers into the room and looks around to see who is screaming. The unaccustomed noise coming from someone she knows well throws her into a panic. Her back and arms go rigid and she starts screaming too. "Aaaaah!" But then she fights off the panic and crawls onto the bed with me.

"Dad, please stop scaring me. I know you don't want to scare me like this." She touches his eyelid and slides his eyes open. Dad's noise gradually subsides, and then he becomes aware of us. He wraps an arm around Linda and looks like he's going to fall asleep again.

"I made you stop screaming," Linda whispers. "I saved you. I'm the hero."

"What the heck was that?" I ask Mom. Now that Dad's quiet you can hear the highway traffic behind the fence. When I slept in their bed as a little kid, that sound was incessant and put me to sleep.

Dad's T-shirt is soggy with sweat.

"That's it," Mom tells Dad, helping him into a dry shirt. Her voice pulses with anger and disappointment. "No more antidepressants."

apprentice

In the studio, Linda primed Dad's canvases for a new group of sunset paintings. She covered each canvas with a layer of tinted gesso so that the paint would stand out better and the backgrounds would have depth. A puddle of newsprint protected the floor. The assembly-line process was interesting, and I felt furtively comfortable watching Linda in this room rather than watching Dad.

"So Linda's been abandoned," I said, leaning in the doorway. "How will she get anything done without someone to discuss it with every nanosecond?"

"Dad's at the beach with his camera while the light is still good." She wore an old dress shirt of Dad's, black-and-white-striped socks, some stretchy red pants that had belonged to our grandmother, Mom's holey Keds, and a beret. Paint spots flecked her whole outfit, even the hat, which made me believe she had put them there intentionally. I could picture her in her room with those clothes spread on the bed, talking to her stuffed

Garfield and flecking furiously like Jackson Pollock.

"That's not what I meant. I meant, where is Jodie? I can't believe she's making you do this by yourself."

Linda frowned at the canvas. Nothing could distract her from this important and potentially profitable work.

"How will you cope?" I needled.

She evened out the coat of paint with a rag. "That's the first time you've missed having Jodie around. I'll have to tell her your feelings about her have changed."

"Really, where is she? I hope she hasn't found another family to glom on to like a barnacle." I laughed a wicked laugh that I've used to torture Linda since she was four and I was seven. This made her look up.

"If you don't like her, why are you even asking?"

"I thought maybe she was smarter than I gave her credit for. That she realized what a disaster this was going to be."

"She'll be here later. We're a team."

"Of courth," I said, imitating Jodie's noodlelike lisp.

That did it. She shot me a cold and withering look. "Why are you still here? Don't you have a class to fail?"

"That's not funny."

"You're supposed to be getting your grades up. I don't have to improve my grades, so I can do whatever I want."

"What an honor. What a big whoop."

"All right, if you have no real reason to be here, just stay where you are, be quiet, and watch the master."

Linda placed the first canvas near an open window to dry. She took a second canvas from the stack against the wall. Dad had already titled each canvas on the back. A note on the front said which tint he wanted for the background. She placed the next canvas on the easel, shook a jar of blue-green gesso, and spread it in one corner with a sponge brush.

"That's actually a nice color," I said.

"Of course it is."

"But getting back to the reason I'm here."

Using a clean rag, Linda wiped a clump from the brush tip.

"Notice my concentration," she said, working into the middle of the canvas.

"What Dad really needs is to be normal. Go to work, come home. Watch TV while eating Fiddle Faddle. Take a walk. Do normal things." What bothered me most about this painting craze was that I had lost my father a second time. After last winter I thought I was getting him back. But when Dr. Fritz suggested painting, Dad slipped away again. I could count on one hand the number of days since then that I considered him normal.

"Dad's a very strong person. You have to be to go through what he did."

"I know that, but this seems so extreme. Can't he be average, even for a little while?"

Linda nodded toward the jar, and without thinking I held it up for her. The apprentice's apprentice. "Nobody wants to be average," she told me.

"But someone has to be. In fact, most people have to. Statistically."

"Only one-third have to. The others are above average and—cloth, please."

Cloth. "Okay. But you see my point."

The canvas was covered. Linda moved it to the window, beside the first coated one.

"I know exactly what your problem is," she continued, looking straight at me.

"What?"

"You're ticked off because you can't paint. Painting is a talent. I inherited it. That's why Dad needs me as his helper."

"I could if I wanted to." I pointed to the pencil notations on the canvas. "Where's the talent in following instructions? This is like paint-by-numbers."

Linda pointed the brush at me as if she wanted to Pollock my face.

I backed off. "Forget it. I don't want to be on your dumb team." On the way to my room, I ignored how dumb that sounded.

team dumb

Dad, Linda, and Jodie seemed happy. Inseparable. A clot, a club, a dizzy beehive.

Dad started calling Linda "Linda-Lou" and Jodie "Ponytail."

As in "Could you get that, Linda-Lou?" and "What do you think, Ponytail?"

Linda and Jodie crawled over each other for a chance to paint.

Paint in the bathroom, on the rugs, and everywhere.

38.

shift 3, november 11. call 18

Listeners. Can I help you?"

Yeah, hi. Just called to talk.

"How are you doing tonight?"

Okay, I guess. A little down.

"I'm sorry to hear that. Would you like to tell me your first name?"

Jenney.

"Hi, Jenney. So, what's going on?"

Margaret caught my eye. She knew I had trouble terminating Jenney's calls. I would have to keep this one short.

I'm having problems with my school situation.

"Sorry to hear that. What's been happening?"

I'm pretty sure I told you before.

"You may have."

But I guess I have to tell you again, so here goes. I was all set with a great college scholarship and getting ready to start school. I was going to study marine biology. But then I had kind of a nervous breakdown and decided that I should take it easy and focus on my emotional issues instead. So I put my plans on hold. In fact, I've put my whole life on hold while I deal with this crisis. And some days are better than others and some are worse. Much worse.

"Wow. It seems like you're dealing with an awful lot there. I'm sorry it's so stressful."

Thanks. Oh, God, I just dumped so much on you. Ugh.

"That's okay. Hey, take a deep breath. That's what we're here for. I'm glad you called."

How glad can you be?

"So, out of all you just told me, what's bothering you the most?"

It's hard to pick out one strand. . . .

"It does sound hard."

Usually I don't think about it much. Usually I live minute to minute, just trying to survive, but it's only when it's quiet that I really have a chance to think, and that's when it hits me: This isn't the way I wanted to live.

"This isn't the way you wanted to live."

That's right.

"How do you want to live?" Funny how the Incomings hardly ever noticed that we repeated their exact words. You would think they would get weirded out and stop talking.

I thought I'd be in school. I gave up my scholarship when I had my breakdown. Now I'm not sure I had to. I know people do it, start school even when they're dealing with emotional problems. And they're living their life at the same time. They find a counselor at school or near school, or they get into a support group. Maybe I don't have to keep seeing Melinda over the next couple of years.

"So you think maybe you didn't have to give up the scholarship."

Not necessarily. But those people—they're superhuman. They're laser-focused go-getters. Bopping into class every day with their homework done and their clothes just right and their hair looking great and all their problems put aside.

The Generic Laughing People. She meant they had them in college, too.

"And you're not a go-getter?" I asked, checking the clock. Only two minutes so far. I would impress Margaret by bringing this baby in under four.

Not really. I was once. In high school. The whole package. Have you ever looked back on something you've accomplished and said, "How did I do that?"

"Sure," I told Jenney. When I saved my father's life, I thought.

You have?

I caught myself. "I mean, sure, I understand what you're saying."

How did I do the academics and the student government and the music—

"What kind of music?"

Clarinet—

"Go on."

—and the swimming and . . . You know, I have a trophy and everything. You can see it right there in the lobby. And I think, "How did I do all that? Was I some kind of robot?"

"Is it possible that you're being a little hard on yourself?"

Maybe.

"Are you feeling suicidal, Jenney?" The question came much easier now. It was standard, like asking supermarket customers if they wanted a receipt or hamburger purchasers if they wanted fries.

No.

"So, you were a swimmer?"

Yep.

"Do you swim anymore?"

Not in a pool, not to train. I don't even belong to the Y anymore. I swim back and forth at the beach as much as I can. From May to October, anyway.

"It must be cold this time of year."

I wear a wetsuit.

"I admire how you've kept your life together, Jenney."

I haven't, though.

"From the outside it looks like you have."

That's funny. From the inside it looks like there's no life for Jenney.

"What would you most like to change?" It was time to get her thinking positively, solving her own problems. End the call on an up note.

Get started with school. But I won't talk about that now. That's a plan for another day. A go-getter day.

"Speaking of going, I should go in a minute. Jenney."

I feel better having talked to you.

"Good."

I don't know why, though. She laughed a little there.

"It's the Listeners Magic," I said.

It is magic, isn't it?

"Yes, it is. Good-bye, Jenney."

Good-bye. Billy.

Three minutes and forty-eight seconds. Margaret put her hand over the mouthpiece of her phone. That had been a beautiful call on my end, she said. It could be used in a training video, because I had been nearly perfect.

self-evaluation

Margaret was wrong—I hadn't been perfect. Because I forgot to say my name. Let me state my feeling about that: bad. But Jenney said my name, my important name, without my telling her. Let me state my feeling about that: good. Out of all the volunteers she's talked to here, she recognized my voice. And she could have pretended to forget me the way I pretended to forget her, but she decided not to.

40.

and I found myself thinking about her

We were swimming in cold water and shivering and patting each other with towels. I was shivering, she was stealing my towel, and I was chasing her until I felt warm again. We were riding bikes over the bridge between Hawthorne and Beauport, the sails on the water like white slanting As for our excellence. We were feeding each other shoestring potatoes from a tiny bag.

41

L is for laughter

I carried my bike into the bedroom and walked into the kitchen to find a soda. I felt good about my shift. Not only was I perfect, or nearly perfect, on that one call with Jenney, but in four hours I took thirty-one calls, although Pep says I should be in the forty range, including breaks and paperwork. Richie reminded me that the key to terming was emphasizing the quality of your listening, not the quantity.

Dad was at the kitchen sink, wiping his hands with a rag. While his back was turned, Linda came in holding her fingers to form the letter *L*, snapping her head side to side and mouthing "Listerine."

"Cut it *out!*" I yelled. I spiked my empty soda can into the recycling bin to make it clatter. "I was perfect tonight! Nearly perfect!"

"What's up with you two?" Dad asked.

"She's calling me Listerine again!"

"I didn't call him that. I didn't call him anything! I only implied it!"

"Well, stop implying it," Dad said, accusing both of us in one glance. "This conflict is so unnecessary."

"She's driving me crazy, Dad."

"Linda, stop driving your brother crazy. Billy, don't be such a hothead. You can't let people push your buttons like that."

Dad went back to the studio, and the smell of paint thinner rode Handel's Air, a stately tune like a wedding march, into the living room. Was he blasting his music to get inspired, or to drown us out? *Push your buttons.* If I were a father, I would have explored, not dismissed, my son's experience.

Andy texted me to see if I wanted to go to a movie. His treat. He had gotten a gift card for his birthday.

"Busy," I texted back. Yeah, right. Like I wanted to spend a minute more with that idiot than I had to.

I opened my computer to start my music paper and other homework but found myself on the Hawthorne High Facebook page. *Should I look?* I wondered. Should I look up the class of 2010 and swimmers? Nobody would find out, and it would be nice to feel closer to a girl who thought I was good at something. But no, I decided. Who Jenney was outside of that six-inch beige plastic box was none of my business.

think small

When I got up the next morning I found Dad in his studio, already working on the show. He said he had been up since five mulling over more ideas and that he planned to finish another painting before he went to work.

"This level of intensity will help keep *Forty/Forty* from being run of the mill," he told me.

"Have you eaten breakfast?" I asked. I had a bowl of oat squares with me and was careful not to drip milk on anything.

"What people are looking for in art is not a particular subject or style, but excitement," he said. "That's part of my one day, one painting plan. The viewer can tell whether you maintained a level of engagement while painting or whether you finished the piece while deciding what you would have for lunch."

"Okay, Dad. I realize that it's mundane of me to need to feed myself." I pointed to the three finished sunset paintings resting on the pink table from Grandma Pearl.

"Were these exciting?" I asked him. They were gray, after all.

"I was in a state of constant tension: Will I be able to fulfill my vision? Am I going to disappoint myself? In a way it's almost like a sport—skiing or luge—because your success can be due to timing. If you make the wrong decision at a key moment, the whole painting can be thrown off. But if you hit it right, the excitement keeps building right up to the finish."

Dad's told me his next project was a group of very small works. He showed me the canvases. "The small scale is a challenge to people like me who prefer to work large. What can I possibly say in a space like eight by ten inches?"

Linda had heard me getting my breakfast. She came in wearing her Justin Bieber nightshirt. "I love the small idea," she said. "A small painting is the perfect Christmas gift. It doesn't cost a lot, and the person you give it to can always find a place to hang it."

"That's my girl," Dad said. "You'll be working on Wall Street someday."

While he talked, Dad sketched the outlines of a scene he must have come across while walking on the wharf, of a boat being repaired. I guessed it was what you would call Impressionism, because he was trusting the viewer to fill in all the missing parts. He painted the water, the people in the boat, and the name on the transom of the boat. Everything but the boat itself. The people were floating on the water.

"Neat," Linda said. "It's a transparent boat, like the emperor's new clothes."

"What is the name of this one?" I asked.

"*The American Health Care System*," he said.

shift 4, november 15. call 24

Listeners. Can I help you?"

It's Jenney.

"Hi, Jenney. It's Billy. Glad you called."

This is really difficult.

"Take a deep breath. No rush. I'll wait till you're ready to talk. What's going on?"

I heard from my parents again.

"Breathe."

It was awful. And I feel bad but I don't, because I don't think it was my fault. Wait. That didn't make sense.

"What happened?"

They're going after Melinda.

"Okay."

We had a huge argument.

"About Melinda?"

Right. They said she ruined their relationship with me and she should have her license taken away.

"They said that?"

I feel like they're blaming me and it makes me feel bad.

"Did they say that?"

Sorry. I can't talk. The soft clicking noise is back again.

"That's okay. Breathe."

When my parents come at me with this stuff they make me feel guilty, like I'm the one causing the problems. And if I tell Melinda that, she says, "Don't let them make you feel guilty. You don't have to protect them anymore, Jenney." And do you know what is one of the worst things about all that's happened? I lost my mother. I lost both parents, but I especially miss my mother. Even though I'm nineteen, I still need her, you know?

For the second time I almost regretted being at Listeners. Because if I had met Jenney some other way, we'd have a lot to talk about right now. We'd sit in a park somewhere and she'd tell me about losing her mother over the lawsuit, and I'd tell her about having lost my dad even though he was right there in the house with me.

"What do you miss about her?" I asked.

It didn't used to be like this. She was more my friend than my mom. When my acceptance to St. Angus's came we had this day together. We went to Boston and saw the Aquarium, and she joked that once I finished school these people had to fear for their jobs. And we stood at the top of the Giant Ocean Tank and she linked her arm in my arm—we hooked our elbows together, like two old ladies—and we had this feeling of satisfaction. We both did, the exact same feeling, and . . .

She was crying again. My throat tightened, and my nose even started to tingle, as if I might cry myself.

"It's okay," I said. "You can cry if you want to."

Jenney's sadness tumbled out, years' and years' worth it seemed, in her tears.

I don't understand how my life got to be such a mess.

I looked over my shoulder. Margaret and Richie had been called away by one of the college guys. He was saying he was worried about CIA Debra and that if they heard from her, they should tell him right away. My mind was made up before I even knew what I was considering.

I'm sorry, I—

"Jenney, I remember you."

What? Are you whispering?

"I said I remember you."

I knew that. I knew you did.

"Good."

Give me a minute.

"No rush."

My timing was perfect. Margaret and Richie were back at our table. They had written a note to me about CIA Debra that they intended to show me when I got off the phone. I felt both wrong and right. I was closer to someone than I had been in a long time. I knew my breaking the rules had comforted Jenney. It seemed like the rules had been made for someone else, not two people in our situation. Who had so much in common. Maybe the rules were wrong.

Just a minute.

I heard snuffling on the other end. She blew her nose and, I think, walked across the room to throw away the tissue. It seemed intimate to hear, like I was hearing her in the bathroom.

"You're a strong person, Jenney," I said.

I know. On my good days, few can defeat me.

Margaret glanced over. She probably remembered my last, near-perfect call with Jenney. I was coasting on my reputation now.

"Are you feeling suicidal?"

No.

"I'm sorry things are rough."

I'll get through it somehow.

"I know you will. I have to go soon."

Me too. I have to let Melinda know what's happening.

"If you think that's best."

Thanks, Billy.

"Good luck."

'Night.

44.

outside

Dad set up an easel in the backyard, under an almost-bare maple tree. When the wind blew, one remaining clump of leaves fluttered to the left, then to the right, like a pom-pom. A transistor radio on the wooden chair beside him played Handel's *Largo*, drowning out the sound of highway traffic. Painting outside is called painting *en plein air*, French for "in the open air." Yet eating outside is called dining *al fresco*, which is Italian for "in the fresh air." Can you paint *al fresco* or dine *en plein air*? Possibly, but no one ever says that.

I walked up beside Dad and touched his arm, wanting a closer look. He had drawn a scene with pencil, and now he was starting to fill in the colors. When he was sick, I had touched him as much as I wanted. He moved a lot slower then, and he even held my arm sometimes, for support.

"A spy!" he yelled. "Tell me who sent you!"

He wore a paint-splattered hockey jersey. His straw

hat was like Monet's, but his red hair was getting long in back, and with his red goatee and bony face, more than any other artist he resembled Van Gogh. He wiped his brush with a rag and pretended to stab me with it, forcing me to back off. But not before I got a glimpse of his painting, which was . . . odd. Dad's tree had a rubbery face like the trees that come to life in the movie version of *The Wizard of Oz* and try to snatch Dorothy and her friends. But at the base of the tree were carloads of tourists with cameras and binoculars.

"What, exactly, does that represent?" I asked him.

"The attempted rape of New England by the tourist industry."

"It doesn't look like the rape has been very successful," I said. "Are you happy with the work you're doing?"

"Ecstatic," he said. "Sometimes you have a vision and in between the vision and the execution a shadow falls. But not this time. It's turning out exactly the way I imagined it."

"The tree grabbing the cars like King Kong and dumping the tourists into the oncoming traffic? Are the tourists at the bottom of the ravine dead?"

"All the tourists are going to be dead," Dad explained. "What I'm happiest with is this kind of cartoony look that makes you go, 'Oh, what a cute painting of a tree,' and then you look closer and say, 'Uh-oh, not so cute.'"

"I like the fall colors, anyway."

"Luscious colors," Dad corrected. "In art school we called that 'color porn.' It's easy to like color."

He and Linda should just make a dunce cap that says

ART IGNORAMUS and have me sit under it. It would be an artistic dunce cap, I'm sure.

I raised my eyebrows at Dad. He might call me shallow, but I would still push my point. "If you like what you've done so far," I said, "think how much happier you'll be with what you can accomplish a year from now. You'll have a neat collection of work that you've created at a comfortable pace, and you can put more thought into what you want to include. You said you'd do forty paintings in forty days, but you're not locked into that by anyone but yourself." What I really wanted to tell him was that he would still be a great dad even if he finished zero paintings. That if he decided not to finish this marathon, I would love him just the same.

Dad mixed a bronzy color on his palette. It might have contained some actual metal flakes. "How is your project going?" he asked. "I'll bet you're good at it."

This surprised me. In a way I thought Dad had forgotten. "People say I'm good. A couple of the callers say I'm the best Listener they've spoken to." Oops. That was actually a breach of confidentiality.

"It's not too depressing, is it? I worry about you getting depressed. Because"—he looked from the canvas to me—"you know, it could be in the genes. Something undesirable I've given you. At least Linda got my painting ability as a trade."

I wanted a positive souvenir gene too. People always said we looked alike, and both Dad and I bounced when we walked. I wished that for one day I could be not myself but an observer, so I could see it.

"Listeners isn't depressing," I assured him. "The whole

environment is very upbeat. We make jokes and eat snacks and stuff. I've made a couple of friends there."

"Do you feel like you're developing your skills?" Dad asked, squinting at me from under his hat. I noticed that he applied the paint thickly, in pasty waves, where I would have obsessively painted every leaf.

"It's amazing," I said, watching his hands move over the canvas. "I've learned so much about sympathy and about communication. And the secret lives people lead, that otherwise I would know nothing about. I learn something new every time I step through the door."

"Then how would you feel if I did to you what you've been doing to me?"

"Meaning?"

"If I suggested you wait a year before trying to save someone."

"Touché," I said. "I did not see that coming."

Dad was smiling the semi-angry smile of someone with a lot more to say. I ambled back to the house with my head down, acting more wounded than I felt. And I slammed the screen door loudly. This had worked when I was little to convey sulking and hurt feelings. But now when I looked over my shoulder, Dad hadn't seemed to notice.

I continued to watch Dad through the tiny metal squares. Working below the tree, Dad bent his head back like he was drinking from a goblet, filling his eyes and mouth with the colors and textures of the tree bark and sky. He scrutinized the canvas on his easel and turned it upside down. This surprised me. He thought checking a composition by upending it was pretentious. That was one of the reasons he left art school.

Dad turned the canvas upright. He waved and laughed. He had done that for my benefit. Caught me looking, I guess.

director

Paint in the bathroom, on the rugs, and everywhere.

But Mom didn't seem to mind.

Last year she needed tons of time off. Now it seemed she was making up that time and determined, like Dad, never to be average again. In the evenings, while Dad worked in the studio, Mom fanned out her spreadsheets and binders. Her museum was devoted to the leather industry, but the way she acted you'd think she ran the Louvre. She told me not to interrupt her, and once, after I bothered her three times in a row, she came home wearing earbuds. Earbuds on my mother. She always told me to take mine off. Hers lasted one evening and then disappeared, but they drove the point home. No interruptions: this means you, Billy.

I decided to take my homework in there, sit beside her, and wait for a chance to catch her without the headphones.

"The painting Dad's working on looks mental," I said, just to open up the topic.

"I know you're against the show," she said.

"I'm not against the show. I'm just against this format. Don't you think it's too much?"

Mom raked the arm of her eyeglasses through her hair. Sometimes this meant she was thoughtful. Other times it meant she was mad. Which would it be?

"All art is too much," she said in the tone of someone who had a master's degree in American studies.

"What do you mean?" I asked.

Mom touched her hair. She had been wearing it up lately, with a fancy clip, and she wore Mom jeans tucked into a pair of suede boots she was proud of. She looked nice, but I didn't want to change the subject by saying so. She tilted her head and paused, as if she was giving a press conference.

"Any artist who creates something takes a risk," she said. "Of being laughed at or of making something no one else will value. So if that happens to your father, it will be the same as with any other artist. I'm sure that, having a formal art education, he's well aware of the risk and has decided to proceed anyway. Maybe he's even enjoying that aspect of it, because it's like the good old days when he pursued his art against the odds."

Having stated her point, to her mind, perfectly, Mom started inspecting a set of slides. She wanted to expand the museum's scope from the merely local. She hoped to display, in an unprecedented coup, a collection of traditional Plains Indian leather pipe bags from a museum in South Dakota. She held each slide toward the lamp, unconsciously drawing her mouth into an upside-down U.

"So you don't think that if his show bombs or doesn't happen, he'll be crushed?"

She laughed. "Of course not. He'll be happy."

"What if he doesn't get the forty paintings done? He'll be happy with failure?"

"Happy at having made an attempt." She grimaced at another slide. "He's busy and he's happy. That's what we wanted, right? End of story."

46.

soaring

It seemed that every time I tried to get closer to Dad I was rebuffed. I had to put my personal feelings aside, though. What was more important was to follow up on my suspicion: that Dad was getting sick in the opposite direction of last year. Last year he was down and hopeless and had no energy. This year he was up and energetic and had too much hope. There had to be a relation between the two. The not eating or sleeping, the constant working, and especially the complete lack of judgment on the quality of his work.

I looked in *Your Mental Health* for something that matched Dad's symptoms and found Chapter 2, "Euphoric or Irritable Mood." The authors said that anyone taking antidepressants had to be careful of irrational happiness ("hypomania") because it could lead to bipolar disorder and a lifetime of cycling up and down. Had Dr. Gupta and Dr. Fritz warned Dad about this? The hell with the doctors. Mom had been stupid to trust them again.

Too impatient to read the entire chapter, I Googled "bipolar disorder" and found the National Institute of Mental Health website listing "symptoms of a manic episode":

MOOD CHANGES

- A long period of feeling "high," or an overly happy or outgoing mood
- Extremely irritable mood, agitation, feeling "jumpy" or "wired"

BEHAVIORAL CHANGES

- Talking very fast, jumping from one idea to another, having racing thoughts
- Being easily distracted
- Increasing goal-directed activities, such as taking on new projects
- Being restless
- Sleeping little
- Having an unrealistic belief in one's abilities
- Behaving impulsively and taking part in a lot of pleasurable, high-risk behaviors, such as spending sprees, impulsive sex, and impulsive business investments

Dad had them all, except maybe irritability. And I didn't know, or want to know, about his sex life.

So Mom, Dad, Linda, and Jodie all thought what Dad was doing was fine. Maybe I couldn't get in the way of Dad's forty days. But I could be his guardian. I could hover over Dad and the show.

shift 5, november 18. call 29

Listeners. Can I help you?"

"Hello . . . *Hello?*"

No response from the other end, but no dial tone either. The caller was still on the line.

"Hello? This is Listeners."

Uh.

A strangled, grunting sound. Why wasn't the caller speaking? My heart pounded. Oh my God, was this a Likely? Margaret and Richie were both on calls. I grabbed my manual and my list of emergency numbers, which, like everything else on the table, suddenly looked unreal and faraway. I tugged Richie's sleeve. I made my eyes huge and pointed at my handset. Richie mouthed the word *Likely?* and I raised my eyebrows and nodded. Richie touched Margaret's arm, but she raised a finger to put him off.

"Are you all right?" I asked the caller.

Uh. Sorry. Swallowing the tail end of my sandwich.

"How're you doing this evening?"

Not too great. My girlfriend dumped me.

"I'm sorry to hear that."

No, actually it was good news.

"Oh, why's that?"

I kinda pushed her into it. By, you know, stepping out with other ladies.

"But you weren't happy in this relationship, it sounds like."

Not at all.

"So you said you weren't feeling great."

I have some dental problems too.

"That sounds rough."

I'm on painkillers.

"Do they help?"

Pretty well. You know, I talked to you before.

"Really?"

Yeah. I recognize your voice.

"Maybe. I'm not sure."

No, I'm sure I do. We talked last week. I'm Matt. It's Billy, right?

"Yes."

We just talked, like, a few days ago.

"We get a lot of calls here. So, tell me more about your dental pain. How long have you had it?"

I told you that last time. Don't you remember?

"No, I'm sorry."

Do you have early Alzheimer's or something?

"Are you feeling suicidal?"

No. Ha! You asked me that last time.

"So how are you coping, with the pain and all?"

Matt needed oral surgery, but it was expensive and his dad's insurance policy wouldn't pay for it. So he kept taking higher doses of painkillers, which made him logy, and he had fallen asleep at the wheel today. Rather than offer advice, I encouraged him to tell me his options and decide for himself which sounded best. I added heaps of reflective listening about the pain. I was good at this. I was very good.

on hold

I pressed hold.

I slid the manual to the table's edge and let it fall on the floor.

One of the college kids came in from the front room to raid the snack cabinet. He found a bag of trail mix and did an end-zone dance with the bag on his way out.

I wish I would get a Likely, I told Richie. The words sounded morbid coming out of my mouth, but they were true. If all I did was listen and never take action, I was no better than a Listerine.

Richie pointed his thumb at the front room. Those guys got the Likelies, he told me. Mostly on the weekends, during overnights. The overnights were grueling, he said. Around two in the morning the Listeners in that room would do anything to stay awake. Last Saturday they had ended up having races in the chairs.

That sounded fun, I said. I realized I sounded both pathetic and young, but Richie was probably thinking the same thing. I yearned to roll my office chair across the room, from end to end of the phone bank, spinning in circles and making a thundering noise.

Someday that would be us, Richie said.

life saver

Richie checked the cabinet to see if the large foraging primate had left us anything. Margaret looked a little zoned out. Richie asked why she was so quiet.

A Likely, she said.

While Richie and I were talking. Goddamn it! It was fate, the spin of the roulette wheel. Because she was line 1 and I was line 3, she had gotten a Likely while I'd gotten a guy with bad teeth. How long would it be now, how many weeks or months, before another Likely called?

Richie asked if the caller was one of our regulars.

It was a brand-new Incoming, Margaret told us. An elderly man named Hagrid.

What was the suicide plan? I asked.

Hagrid had been about to jump off a building. He had been standing right on the ledge, talking to her on his cell phone. She could hear the wind and the cars. He was four stories up and described the people on the ground shouting. The whole scene.

Hagrid was certainly an unusual name, I said.

Richie's lips moved during Margaret's recap. He repeated almost every word Margaret said, as if it was his own call. The scene seemed real to him, even though he had only heard it from Margaret, who heard it from the Incoming.

Margaret said she felt like she had just done the special job she was put on earth to do. She felt almost a little high.

The call would have been pretty convincing except for the stupid name. Too bad for Margaret. She didn't get my Likely after all. But I didn't want to burst Margaret's bubble. She looked illuminated, like she'd just stepped out of church.

I asked her what else happened in the call, and Margaret said she had talked him off the ledge. Richie repeated her words again, passing a bag of trail mix.

Right at the end, Hagrid had a change of heart. When he said he was intent on killing himself, she asked him if he could wait until tomorrow. And then he said it was all too much trouble and he had changed his mind. And he made this little jumping sound—a sound of exertion, and she didn't know if he was on his way to the pavement or what—but he said he had jumped back inside the building. Margaret felt so proud. She wished she could tell her parents what she did. Or at least her cousin who was a priest.

But she couldn't because of confidentiality, I said. That's a shame.

Margaret sat perfectly still, as if having saved someone's

life, she saw no need to ever move again. The phones were flashing, but none of us felt ready to take a call.

I said finally that it seemed kind of weird, that a ninety-year-old man would be so nimble, jumping on and off ledges.

That wasn't so unusual, Richie explained. Plenty of eighty-five- and ninety-year-olds climbed mountains and ran marathons.

Margaret raised her head, and I realized she had been praying. She went to the front room so Pep could debrief her about the call.

fractured

When I got home Dad was finishing another painting in the fruit-bowl series. The new painting showed the earth split in two like a coconut. The pieces sat in what looked like a woven basket, but when you looked closely the strands were human fingers. The title was *Who Will Re-pair?* Jodie and Linda oohed over the details. Jodie's barrette dangled from two strands of hair like an oversize zipper.

I pictured people coming in to the show and trying to make sense of this. I didn't want Dad to be judged. By anyone. He was foolish to get his opinions from two silly girls.

Nor did I want him judged for what happened in the winter. It was one thing for me to know something was wrong with Dad—that was necessary for getting the problem solved. It was another thing for people outside to know.

He was my dad, after all. He was Bill Senior. And I was Bill Junior.

muses

Mr. Gabler stopped by my desk, waiting. But I had nothing.

"What is the problem this week?" he asked. "I gave you some leeway. This is a real failure to execute."

How could I muff that assignment again? It wasn't even that difficult. I could have done it in fifteen minutes. But for the second class in a row I'd spaced out.

"What was that all about?" Gordon asked me after class. He gets superb grades without appearing to try. He hardly ever mentions the work, but he never misses an assignment.

Of all the people in the world, Gordy was definitely someone who could be trusted with the truth. "My dad wants to have an art show," I told him.

"Why are you telling me this like it's bad news?"

"It seems unrealistic," I said. "I think he might be"—I turned around to face him so I can speak in a lower voice—"getting sick again."

"Sick how?" Gordon asked. His expression: face very

straightforward, almost at military attention, and lips kind of pursed together to make sure no sound of his own squeaked out. It was the visual equivalent of Richie's listening voice, and I felt for that minute like I was the most important person in Gordy's world.

"Do you know what bipolar disorder is?" We were at his locker, number 217, and I stared at the front of 219 while I said those words. That Gordy would know something about Dad that Dad didn't know himself—it was like one of those hospital gowns that open in the back, so everyone but you knows that your rear end is showing. It was humiliating.

"I know some people who've been diagnosed with it," Gordy said, digging out his lunch bag and a five-dollar bill. I wondered if he meant Brenda. But I didn't push.

"I've been reading up on it," I said. I turned my head and met Gordy's eyes. "Some people don't start out bipolar, but if they're depressed and start taking antidepressants in too high a dosage, they can become manic. Then they spend the rest of their lives swinging from one extreme to the other."

"You think that's happening to your dad?" We walked into the courtyard. Some of the granite slabs in the ground around the school were so huge that the builders decided to just leave them there, creating an open space in the middle of the buildings. On sunny days the stone got warm by lunchtime. It felt *rewarding* to sit on, the way a stone summit felt when you reached it during a summer hike. There were benches, too, but we sat on a rock to finish our conversation.

"It might be. My mom isn't picking up on it. I'm a little surprised, because she's usually really skeptical about drugs."

"Does he need the drugs?"

"I think so. He dropped them last winter, and it was a bad scene. You remember."

Yes, he did. If I was Dad's caregiver, Gordy had been mine. It was Gordy who bought me a cheese-steak sub when my whole family was undernourished, Gordy who covered me with a blanket while I napped or cried on his living room couch, and Gordy who took me to a Buddy Guy concert in Boston when I needed to run away from home.

"What makes you think he's manic?" We both watched the tennis courts now, and that made it easier to talk. A girl from music history class was walking onto the court with her friend. The stood at the net, deciding who would serve. The red-haired one passed the balls to the dark one, and they linked pinkies for a few seconds before starting the game.

The facts sounded innocuous. I dropped my voice to make the point. "He's painting all the time."

Gordy waited.

"Okay, and there's more to it than that. He's spending too much money and has an unrealistic sense of his own abilities. And when I say he's painting all the time, I mean with every free minute and giving up sleep to do it. He's going to make forty paintings in forty days and then display them and invite, I don't know, the MFA or Channel 7 News."

"You care about your dad a lot, don't you?" Gordy said.

I nodded. I couldn't say anymore, so I squeezed Gordy's arm. We heard the *thwop-thwop* of the tennis ball, like a metronome, and the girls' laughter after each point.

52.

meter

Andy was waiting for me in the lunch line.

"'S'up, Hagrid?" I asked, knocking him on the shoulder. He almost fell into the tray caddy, and I was surprised by my own force.

Andy pressed his back against the wall. "I see cars down there," he said in an ancient, wheezing voice. "I see little tiny people. I'm just going to jump and end it all!"

"Stop laughing, Andy. She's my friend, and you hurt her."

"She's an acquaintance. I'm your friend." He smiled as if he had grappled me, or perhaps Margaret, into submission.

"The meter could be running out on that." The lunch line took three steps forward.

"I didn't hurt anyone," he said, still teetering and talking in his old-man voice. "It was funny."

I grabbed a tray. I wanted to shove him into the tray caddy and bash my tray over his head. "She's my friend, and you made a fool of her," I said. My voice got conspicuously loud, and I had to remind myself that this business was confidential. "I can't say too much, but you should have seen how happy she was after that call."

"Okay. I made someone happy." Andy walked up to the food lady and ordered the sloppy joe. "And it was still funny," he added.

"It was not funny."

Being short, Andy usually had excellent posture. It was only tall guys who had the luxury of slouching. I felt myself straighten up. Adrenaline charged into my shoulders and upper arms. Andy's gaze fell to my chest. Ray, the guy who set up the steam tables, was looking there too. I realized that I was making a fist.

"Are you planning to hit me?" Andy asked, talking in his own voice again.

"Of course not. I don't hit people. You want to be a fool, be a fool." I pushed him ahead in the line and ordered a sloppy joe for myself. "But don't make a fool of other people."

the g word

A bright November day. Through the screen door, I saw
Mom and Dad taking a break in Mom's rose garden.
Mom had neglected the garden last year, so this year she
made the most of it. Everything was raked and dead-
headed and pruned. Each rosebush had its own square,
cut into the grass and lavished with manure. A statue
of Athena, goddess of wisdom, presided in the middle,
and two or three flowers had lasted into November.
Although the neighbor's leaf blower sounded like a
burping machine gun, Mom and Dad, in their white
plastic stackable chairs, drinking store-brand diet cola,
apparently thought they were in paradise. When the
blower stopped you could hear the Asianlike tone of a
wind chime.

Dad removed his straw hat and leaned over Mom's
chair, hiding both their faces with the hat while he kissed
her. When he had disappeared to the front of the house,
I approached her.

"Mom," I asked in a low voice, "how many of the paintings have you actually seen?"

"Two or three," Mom said. She leaned back in her chair to get the sun on her face. Disturbingly, she was still smiling from Dad's kiss.

I moved Dad's chair so my mouth would be close to Mom's ear. "Have you seen the one of the whale trying to swallow another whale headfirst, so they both get stuck and have to stay that way forever? Don't tell me that's not the product of a fevered imagination."

Mom's red lipstick stretched in a laugh. "I didn't quite get that one either."

"Does anyone get it, other than Dad? I think he has a secret system of meanings that's all in his head."

Mom squeezed my hand, and I felt some of the affection from Dad squickily transfer to me. "Maybe he's an unrecognized genius. Not everyone will get or like what he's doing. How do you think most middle-class Spaniards reacted when they first saw Dalí's *Persistence of Memory*?"

"Which one is that?"

"With the melting watches."

"I call that one *Melting Watches*."

"Your dad might be ahead of his time," Mom said. She flicked a beetle off one of the flowers. Mom wasn't really a reliable judge of anything. She was just in love with Dad.

dislocation

So, what would be my role for the show? I would monitor it and make sure Dad didn't go off the rails. Unless I was at school or Listeners, I made a point of being close by for every major discussion or decision.

I stopped at the house before my Listeners shift and found Dad designing a poster for the show while his brother Marty looked over his shoulder. Of the two of them, Marty was the sociable schmoozer. Marty owned a bar/restaurant and knew a lot of people in town. He had a full head of blow-dried hair and always ironed his jeans before wearing them.

"I can't wait to get the word out," he told Dad. "I'll stand on the street corners if I have to."

I looked over Dad's shoulder at his iPad. In white type on red, the poster said

BILL MORRISON 40/40
Forty Paintings in Forty Days

"Where's the ticket price?" Linda asked. "Real museums charge admission."

"But galleries don't," Dad replied. "Besides, I'm an unknown."

"Don't put yourself down, Dad," Linda argued. "You have the same right to be famous as anyone else."

"I know. But the word 'unknown' isn't negative. It's neutral. Let's say I'm not known yet."

"That's better."

Dad popped different images into the poster to see which looked best. He tried *Diverted Horizon,* in which the horizon line was six inches higher on the right than on the left; *Adverted Horizon,* which contained an entire sunset inside a hyperrealist beer stein; and *Perverted Horizon,* one of the paintings in black and gray.

"It looks like the moon setting," Linda said. "Except that the moon doesn't set. Does it?"

"Do you think it does?"

"I guess so. But no one ever talks about it."

"That's the whole point of the painting. The major objective in art is to avoid clichés."

Linda was writing ideas on a clipboard. "We should serve hot chocolate and offer a gift-wrapping service to put people in a buying mood."

"I can make bows," Jodie said, writing on the clipboard from the other side.

"Of courth you can," I said.

"What do you mean, of course?" she asked.

"Because it's just the kind of thing you would do. Something that looks sweet and nice but is actually useless."

"Cool it, Billy," Uncle Marty said. He laid his arm across the top of the couch, behind Dad's shoulders.

Dad looked up at me. "I will not allow you to use my show as an opportunity to be cruel."

"But don't you think the commercial stuff will make your show seem tacky?"

"No, I don't think. I'm glad for the help. And I'm going to give Linda a percentage on everything she helps me sell. And Jodie a percentage on the gift wrapping."

"Are you going to get a credit card reader?" In case anyone thought I was serious, I snorted.

Dad handed the iPad to Marty, and I knew I was in trouble. "Now listen up, Billy, because I'm only saying this once. You know all about listening, don't you?"

Not that again.

"This show—Billy, look at me—this show is one of the four most exciting events of my life. The other three were my marriage to your mother and the births of my two children. Are you putting that in perspective?"

I looked down at my feet. If Dad had continued in a teasing vein, I could have gotten more potshots in. But he had me cornered. "Yes, I am," I said.

"I'm not fabricating that. It's the truth. It's what I've told Fritz. So now you know. And no naysayer is going to make it less than it is. You seem pretty risk averse, Billy."

"Billy has a lousy attitude," Jodie said, hitching a free ride on the reprimand.

"Okay, Jodie," Dad said. "That's too personal. I want to design my poster, not referee your arguments."

"You've surrounded yourself with yes men, Dad," I

said. "If you told these three you were going to make a rink back there, wear a skating costume, and call the show Bill Morrison on Ice, they'd say it was a great idea."

"Billy," Marty said. "Now you're being offensive."

"What if it snows? What if there's a sleet storm or an ice storm and the art gets ruined? What if there's a blizzard and no one comes? What happens to your precious art show then?"

"There's something you'll need to learn for your career as a musician, Billy," Dad said.

"I'm not a musician. I'm a psychologist. Going to be."

"Whatever you become, this skill might come in handy. It's called improvising. Going with the flow. Deciding in the moment. That's what I'm doing now. Life is full of the unexpected, and the best thing we can do is embrace it. Success is determined by a combination of planning and improvising. Let this show be an example to you."

The four of them went back to fine-tuning the poster and deciding what they could sell.

It was like they didn't remember last winter. All of them had been there. We must have had six different plans, each of which we tossed out the window so fast, we didn't hear the previous one shatter on the pavement. And what did I do as each plan failed? I improvised. I came up with new ideas, and when I had no ideas left I stayed there, sitting with Dad. *Listening* to Dad.

They were like drowning people who said to the lifeguard, You can put me down now, here's five dollars for your trouble, and once we're back on shore, we don't know each other.

And that tall chair you sit in, doesn't it lift you a bit too much above the others?

55.

shift 6, november 22. call 31

I was alone in the teen room, sitting in Margaret's spot. Margaret and Richie had stepped out to record voice-overs for a fund-raiser. A lot of rich people, including friends of Pep's dad, would be coming to the Hawthorne Plaza Hotel to eat tiny quiches and drink mojitos. Once they were slightly buzzed and settled at their tables, the lights would go out, and they would hear two voices, a Listener and an Incoming, talking to each other in the dark. The recordings would be really dramatic, Pep had said. A wallet opener. She needed Margaret and Richie for about twenty minutes of script reading.

Line 1 rang.

"Listeners. Can I help you?"

It's me.

Oh, man, it was her. She was okay, and she sounded happy.

"Jenney! Where've you been? I got worried when I didn't hear from you."

I'm sorry. I called a bunch of times, but I always got some- one else, so I hung up. I wish there was some way I could get you directly.

"Me too." I shouldn't have said that.

I have great news!

"What is it?"

I got a job. My friend Stacey is working part time for a catering company. They do clambakes and corporate parties. The woman who owns it used to run that breakfast place The Incredible Egg. They're really busy right now and needed someone who isn't in school, so they hired me.

"That's incredible. Stacey sounds like a good friend."

Yeah. We hadn't been hanging out that much lately. She says she still wants to be friends but she can't deal with me on the really down days. She says I sometimes seem like another person. I told her things would be getting better soon, that I would be more myself.

"Seems like things *are* getting better for you. You found a job. You're amazing."

Ta-da. But wait! There's more.

"Tell me."

Next step is to enroll at the community college. I'm going over there on my lunch break tomorrow to see how many cred- its I can earn that I could carry to a four-year school. Just to get the ball rolling.

"I'm in awe."

It's not St. Angus's. It's not even Hawthorne State. But they have open enrollment, so if I can work around the hours of the new job, I could start in January. I guess that was all I wanted to say. I should go to bed now. I have to get up early to work a breakfast meeting. I'm feeling a little wired. I'm going to take a couple of Ambien.

"Don't go yet. Let's talk for a few more minutes."

Okay. But just a few.

"Do you know you're my favorite caller?"

I think that's really nice. So you don't mind the fact that I'm so messed up?

"I don't look at it that way. I think people who've been through weird stuff are actually stronger than people who haven't been through weird stuff."

Good. Because I think my weird stuff makes me strong too.

I picked up Margaret's pen and added a heart to her doodle pad. Drawing on her paper felt weird, like wearing someone else's underwear or using their deodorant.

Hey, you sound kind of subdued or something. Not my usual Hallmark. Is something bugging you?

"Me? No. Well, kind of, but I'm not here to burden you with my problems."

Go ahead.

"No, really. I should only be listening to you."

You disrespect me by saying that.

"How?"

You're telling me I can only accept help and never give it.

She was right. I was disrespecting her. She was one of the strongest people I knew, and I was treating her like she was weak.

"That wasn't meant to be personal. I . . . okay." I flipped over Margaret's doodle pad to the blank cardboard. "I'm really worried about my dad."

What's going on with him?

"I think he suffers from . . . Excessive Joy Syndrome."

Be serious, Billy. I can handle it.

I whipped around to see if Margaret and Richie had returned from the taping yet. The coast was clear.

"I'll keep it short. He's taken on a huge, impossible project, and I'm worried that he might be getting manic."

What is the project?

"An art show. He's doing all these paintings *plus* investing his entire self-worth in it *plus* spending tons of money on art supplies, and doing it all too fast."

I can see why you'd be upset. Poor Hallmark. You're such a caring person.

"Do you know what I mean by manic?"

Yep. Like bipolar. Not just good days/bad days like I have. More like ecstatic days and end-it-all days.

"My dad was seriously depressed last year and it got really scary. He's my reason for working at Listeners."

Margaret and Richie came back, each holding a flash drive, their faces red from laughing. Margaret told Richie he could get an Oscar for his performance as an Incoming. Richie said it was a hoot to wear the shoe on the other foot. Richie sat down at 2, and Margaret at 3. When I was finished with Jenney, we would reshuffle.

"Jenney, are you feeling suicidal?"

No, Hallmark. Do you believe in soul mates?

"That's a good question. Do you?"

I do. Like kindred spirits. People who have the same outlooks and values.

"What does that mean to you, Jenney?"

Now that you told me about your dad, I like you more than ever.

The line disconnected.

score

Call 36 was a girl whose boyfriend kept trying to break up with her.

I told him I didn't accept it.

She had a snooty, entitled voice.

"You can do that?" I asked her.

Sure. I told him, "Try again next week."

I wanted to say I admired her gumption or chutzpah, but since I had never used either before, the word came out "gumpchah."

My what?

Call 39 was someone who had a virus that threw off his sleep cycle so that he slept all day and was awake at night.

My whole life is upside down. What do you think I'm eating right now, at nearly nine o'clock at night?

"I have no idea."

Guess.

"I'd like to, but I can't."

I am eating Raisin Bran.

By 8:58 I had taken forty calls in a single shift, and Margaret placed a paper crown with the number 40 on my head.

Richie said the occasion called for a snack. We had Mallomars and white grape juice, with seconds and thirds, in perpetuity.

foothold

At the end of the shift Richie and I learned that Vince, a college student who'd covered the nine-to-midnight singlehanded several nights a week, flunked out and moved back home to Rhode Island. His parents went ballistic, and Vince was so distraught, he had started calling Listeners from his childhood bedroom in his parents' house, using our 800 number. Vince called Margaret tonight, in fact. He said he didn't understand what happened, that it was unfair, and that he was thinking of suing the college. She felt sorry for Vince and didn't want to question his reality, but I couldn't help wondering about his judgment and how good a Listener he had been over the past year.

Margaret and Richie left, and I put my phone on hold. Already a light flashed on line 1, meaning a new Incoming wanted to get through. I went to the front room.

I told Pep the lines were still hopping.

Trouble takes no holidays, Pep said. She was getting

ready to leave too, grabbing her peacoat, her book bag, and her squash racket.

It was a shame about Vince, I said.

Pep told me she had gotten Vince a few times. The first time he caught her by surprise, so she was a little ragged, but she managed to say that she admired him for suing Hawthorne State and that it showed a real commitment to getting an education.

That was a reach, I told her, but a good save. I added that if she was struggling with the schedule, I would be glad to pick up some of Vince's hours until she trained more volunteers.

Pep hesitated. She said she was worried about me burning out.

I still felt fresh, I assured her. In fact, I felt like the more I worked, the faster I would develop my skills.

She asked how late I could stay.

Eleven or midnight, I suggested. However late she needed me.

Pep paused, and I knew what she would say: I needed my parents' permission.

I played the age card. Did Pep ask all the Listeners that, or just the younger teens?

Just the younger teens, she admitted.

My parents would be all right, I said. They had their own stuff going on and probably wanted me out of their hair.

She asked if I would be okay working alone, and I said yes.

I would have to tell her if my hours became too much, she insisted, and I agreed.

All right, I said. I would be back in tomorrow.

58.

mom

I brought Triumph inside and switched on the living room light.

"Oh!" Mom said, blinking. She got up from the couch with her hair sticking up like feathers. "Billy. What time is it?"

"Around ten," I told her. "Mom, I got promoted."

"Oh!" Mom's hand flew up and touched her neck, her wooden bead necklace. "Billy!" She did a wriggly dance like the one Linda did when Dad announced his reinvestment in painting. "That's fantastic!"

Mom hugged me. She smelled sweaty from sleeping in her clothes.

"I took your advice. About working twice as hard."

I carried my bike to my room and came back.

"So what does this promotion entail?"

"Working some extra hours. I'll be on by myself some nights. I'll be running the whole place."

Mom put her arm around me and pointed to the

coffee table. It was littered with correspondence, newsletters, and directories. "I'm starting an e-mail discussion list with other directors of small museums," she said. "It was a good idea, but it's taking longer than I thought."

"Is Dad still working?" I asked.

She moved a teacup and put her feet up. "Yes. Go in and tell him. He'll be so proud."

in other words

I pushed open the door of Dad's studio. A new lamp as bright as a klieg light blazed in the midst of the solvent smells, and the air in the room felt like a sauna.

"Little buddy," Dad said. He hadn't called me that since I was four or five. He rested his brush on the easel tray and massaged a sore spot on his shoulder. His current painting was of three white rowboats docked side by side. The third one was barely present, suggested with a scraping of white.

"You're home late. How were the phones tonight?" he asked. I noticed creases around his eyes.

"Busy. I'm going to be spending more time at Listeners, okay? They're shorthanded."

"That's fine. Another hour or two and I can hit the hay, Billaby."

"What boats are those?"

With a clean brush tipped with green paint, he wrote part of an *N* on the middle boat. Then he scraped a *P* onto the nearest one. "Three boats embarking on a dangerous journey. No one knows what's on the other side."

"I get it. The *Niña*—"

"The *Santa María*. The *Pinta*. And the *Niña* in between-ya. One intrepid soul masterminds the journey. He has some idea what's ahead. . . . Almost done, Billaby, almost done. Then one more and we'll say good night."

"Maybe you should sleep in tomorrow and take a sick day. You look wiped out."

"I won't go to bed until I finish one more."

"A small one like this?"

"Maybe I'll make a painting of you. Call it *Issue of My Tissue*. Or I'll paint you in a fruit bowl and call it *Fruit of My Loins*. Get it?"

Dad finished the lettering—just two letters on each stern did the job. "It's important not to make details too complete," he said. "That's the mark of an amateur. I'll do another very small one. If Linda of Finland prices by the minute, it won't be worth more than twenty-five smackeroos. But by other standards it will be worth two hundred. She wants to be fair, does Linda of Finland, Queen of Linland. Linda-Finda of the Fair Hair." He removed the canvas from his easel and set it on the table to dry.

"You didn't know what your old man had in him."

"It—"

"So instead of being fer him, you chose to be agin him."

"Not against you, Dad."

"Agin the show?"

"Against you wearing yourself out."

"You should be fer me, Billymelad. I was always fer you, right, Billaby? Linda's fer me, but not you. You decided to cut the umbillycal cord. Where is your filament, son?"

We were alone on a nighttime island, in a quiet broken by the lamp's *tink* and the rivery rush of traffic. I had nowhere to look but at him and his paintings, and despite what the rest of the family said I knew something was very wrong. I didn't want to stick around and watch this whole thing fall apart. I was glad I had somewhere else to go.

60.

last winter: useless

After Dad wakes up screaming, Mom stops Dad's antidepressants. She even stops his therapy appointments, although Dr. Fritz seems to be a pretty good guy and harmless. When I see Mom cancel the appointments and ignore the ringing phone, I know she is thinking about Grandma Pearl, her own mother, who had died of cancer, and who was sliced and burned and filled with poisons by doctors long after she should have been left alone.

"No more doctors," Mom tells Linda and me. "We're going to take care of Dad ourselves. Billy, I want you to come home directly after school every day and keep your dad company. No friends, no meetings, no movies. Play cards or board games with him or whatever you think will pass the time."

That's right. Mom asks me to babysit my own father.

Dad starts watching *Painting with the Light-Teacher* on public TV. Dad used to revile the Light-Teacher and say he was a complete fraud. Now he follows every brushstroke as if this cheesy guy's some kind of hero.

Dad watches the Light-Teacher paint a bouquet of sunflowers. Then he looks down at his own hands.

"Useless, useless, useless," he says.

shift 7, november 25. call 19

Listeners. Can I help you?"

Yeah.

"How're you doing this evening?"

Not too good.

"I'm sorry to hear that. My name's Billy. Do you want to tell me your name?"

Kevin.

"I'm glad you called, Kevin. So, what's going on?"

I have a lot of guilt.

"About what?"

I stole money from my mom to buy cigarettes.

"And you feel guilty about that."

Yeah. She doesn't have much money.

"It sounds like honesty is really important to you, Kevin. I admire that."

No, it isn't. In fact, my name isn't really Kevin.

call 43

Listeners. Can I help you?"

Hi, Billy.

It's after nine o'clock, and no one else should be around. Still, I close the door between the teen room and the Statie room.

"Jenney—what's going on?"

I just had one of the worst days of my life.

"Are you okay?"

I hate to drag anybody down.

"Drag me wherever you want. That's what I'm here for."

Okay, my two supposed best friends from high school who are both at Hawthorne State and who I haven't hung out with in weeks were supposed to take me to a party at the dorm and I was looking forward to it all week and we were going to meet at this one friend's house and leave together from there. Then they called and said the party was canceled because one of the people throwing the party decided to go home for Thanksgiving and wasn't going to be around. My friends were staying home, so I said I was psyched about getting together with them, so why don't we do something else just to get together, because I haven't seen them for weeks?

"Mm-hmm."

They said let's talk later and I didn't hear back. So I called them both and left messages and said let's just order takeout and play a board game or something—why? because I'm a dork—and we'll chill and catch up the way we used to. So I left a message saying I would pick up the food and treat everybody, and I went to my friend's house—she still lives with her parents—and I'm carrying my board game. *Oh my God, I'm talking so fast. You can guess what happened.*

"No, I can't. You have to tell me."

My friend wasn't there. Because they went to the party. It wasn't canceled.

"How did you know?"

Stacey's parents were home. They told me Stacey and Rebecca went to a party at the college and they, the parents, were sorry I hadn't been able to go. They looked sorry for me, which was uncalled for, and I said don't give it another thought it's just bad timing and when I carried my Scrabble to the car my hands shook and you could hear the letter tiles rattling.

"I wish I could make it better."

Don't pity me, Hallmark.

"You don't want people feeling sorry for you. You have pride. I admire that."

I drove past the campus and saw Stacey and Rebecca walking through the main parking lot with a couple of nice-looking guys and they were all laughing together.

"Mm."

But worst of all, they looked up and saw me and they looked the other way as if they didn't even want to acknowledge me.

"That can't be true."

How do you know it's not true?

"I hope it's not true. Isn't Stacey the one who got you that job?"

But that's different.

"Take a minute, Jenney. Breathe in and out."

I guess I'm just not fun anymore. I never intended to be this person.

"Maybe they didn't even see you in your car."

You think I imagined it?

"Maybe there's some other explanation for why they didn't call you."

What could it be, then?

"Jenney, are you feeling suicidal?"

Not really.

"What does that mean?"

I would say that the distance between what I thought my life would be like two years ago and what it's like right now is so huge, I don't think I could ever cross it. Not ever.

"Not ever?"

No.

"No way, no how?"

No.

"Not even in a hot-air balloon? Or the space shuttle?"

No. And no.

"Sorry. I was trying to make you laugh."

I admire you for that.

"Ouch. Remember that you have someone."

I do, don't I.

"You have us. You have the Listeners."

That's what you meant?

"No. I meant you have me."

I thought you meant that. How's your dad doing? I've been worried about you.

"He's still going ahead with it. He's staying up part of the night painting. He churns out a painting every day, or tries to."

What kind of stuff does he paint?

"Still lifes with a heavy political message no one else would understand. Most of them are sort of grotesque. I think Dad's art might actually be bad. He's operating in a vacuum. He isn't getting any perspective from anyone else, and I'm afraid that when he finally gets a reaction on the day of his show he's going to be in for a surprise. Schlock shock."

That's funny.

"But I'm not laughing."

Me either. I guess I've been in too many situations where I got my hopes up and was disappointed. I completely relate to how your father might feel that day.

"Like, 'We all know something you don't know. And now that you know it too, don't you feel like a jerk?'"

It sounds like if your dad gets embarrassed, you're going to be embarrassed too.

"I am. This event is going to be huge. He's talking about sending out press releases and calling the TV stations. Maybe I'll disappear on an all-day bike ride the day of the show. I'd be glad to miss the whole thing."

You know, if he's humiliated, it doesn't really rub off on you. That's like my mom thinking that every time I fail, it's a reflection on her. She should live for herself, not through me. You should live for yourself too.

"You're right. I need to live for myself. You're really good at this, you know that? I can't believe how well you understand me."

Just returning the favor, Hallmark.

Line 2 lit up again. I had ignored it a few minutes ago. "Will you call back later? I'm here by myself until eleven from now on."

Sure. Maybe I'll eat this takeout. Practice my Scrabble— ha, ha.

"Take care, Jenney."

Bye.

63.

refreshing

In the next hour or so, I got three brand-new Incomings.

One, Marie, was obsessed with the death of a supermodel who had a reality show. Marie actually broke down talking about her, as if they'd been friends. "It sounds like this is going to leave a big hole in your life," I heard myself saying.

Another, Paul, felt guilty because he frequently spied on a fellow student when she got dressed. He had drilled a hole in the dormitory wall and everything.

I'm trying and trying and trying not to look, but sometimes I just can't help myself.

"You're a good person, Paul," I said. "You obviously have a lot of concern for that girl's privacy." Had I gotten so far into the realities of my Incomings that I could flip things around like that?

He vowed to wait at least twenty-four hours before giving in to the urge to peep again.

My third new person was afraid to tell his wife that

he had lost his high-paying job. Therefore he dressed in a suit and tie every morning and drove to a truck stop two towns away, where he lingered over breakfast. Then he spent the afternoon talking to the owner of a model-train shop.

"You have a lot of dignity, Salvatore."

I'm trying, Billy. I'm trying.

Trying is the main thing my Incomings have in common.

But one of these days it's going to catch up with me.

"And what will you do then?"

I'll call you.

Salvatore hung up sounding cheerful. If I wasn't the best one at Listeners, was I at least one of the best?

call 61

"Listeners. Can I help you?"

It's me.

"Oh, good."

I took a nap and I feel much better.

"Great."

I'm curious about you. Did you do well in school?

"When I wanted to."

Me too. I was a superstar among some people who follow academics and swimming. But it's hard to get started again.

"Do you miss school?"

In some ways. I miss being busy. Hey, maybe I could do what you're doing.

"What?"

I could be a Listener as a second job. Although I bet it doesn't pay.

"It's strictly volunteer. Not sure I was supposed to tell you that."

I wouldn't care. I'd like to volunteer at something. Maybe when I'm feeling better. When I'm back in school again.

"You'd be great at this. There's an empty chair here waiting for you."

There is?

"For when you decide to come and volunteer. Right next to me."

That's sweet. I need to make a plan. And I need to just generally do better. Starting tomorrow. Not sleep so much. Not focus so much on what's missing but on what I am and what I have. I know there's a better person inside me, someone I was once or was starting to be, and I need to get back to her. Even if the circumstances are difficult.

There's an empty chair here waiting for you. Right next to me. That's the most suave thing I've ever said. Yet it came out so easily. What could I say next? We can take Incomings for an hour, then get coffee downstairs, jostling the Staties who push ahead in line. I'll buy you a cup, then we'll look in the snack cabinet. We'll eat the last bag of Doritos, one for you and one for me.

First I need to make a picture of that girl in my mind and change myself to get to that. Not just for myself, but for us.

"For us?"

For my two friends, too. They don't want to see me the way I am now. I can see why they get uncomfortable. They probably don't know what to talk to me about. If I was back in school, I would seem more normal.

"The board-game thing?"

Burned into my memory, as the saying goes.

"It really bothered you."

I felt better after we talked.

"That's the whole reason I'm here."

I didn't call to get your pity, you know.

"I know."

I called because it's ten thirty and everyone else my age is doing something fun.

"Everyone but you and me."

So why are you there?

"Because I don't want to go home."

Because of your dad, right? It doesn't bug you to listen to people's problems on a Friday night?

"No. Does it bug you to be telling someone your problems on a Friday night? Sorry. I didn't mean that the way it sounded."

I know. Actually, I'd rather be at that party. It's supposed to take up an entire floor in the dorm. But it probably isn't as good as I imagined.

"Most things aren't."

Anyway, what college guy is going to be interested in someone with my problems?

"I think a lot of guys would like you."

I don't have my act together right now.

"So what?"

Hey, do you go to Hawthorne State?

"I'm sorry, I can't answer that question."

Doesn't matter.

"I hope you find someone you like. Because you deserve someone great. You deserve all the happiness in the world."

It's getting late.

"Yep, I should go. I'm here alone right now, and every phone on the table is lit up."

So you're going to save my chair for me?

"Yes, and I'm going to put a cushion on it so you can be nice and comfy."

What do you look like?

"Does it matter?"

I have a mental picture of you. I see it every time we talk.

"What's that?"

You're the Listener, right? You're Big Ears. A huge pair of ears on two legs.

"I'm flattered."

Really?

"No. Can we get back to talking about you?"

Want to know what I look like?

"No."

Sure?

"No. I mean yes."

I never knew it was possible to hear someone blush over the phone.

"There was a topic thread here, but we seem to have lost it."

I wonder if we knew each other in high school.

"Can you ever really know another person?"

That's deep.

I heard Jenney sip from something. Herbal tea, I figured. Or spring water.

Or maybe you're one Big Ear, shaped like a horn, like one of those old-fashioned record players. Phonographs.

"Victrolas."

Smart boy.

"Smart girl. I have to go. Will you be okay?"

Yeah. Down but not out. I'll handle it. I always do.

"I ad—"

—mire that about you. Good luck with your dad and his crazy pictures. I'll be thinking of you.

"Thanks."

Good night, sweet Hallmark prince.

running

On Saturday, Gordon ran past the mansions of the Back Shore while I rode my bike in loops around him. It was almost sunset, and the clouds and sky were reflected in the fingerprint-like puddles of dead low tide. Out in Hawthorne Harbor a real schooner floated by, its sails bellowing gracefully in and out like the dome of a jellyfish.

My tires hissed in the wisps of sand along the road. I looped back to my friend with a purpose in mind.

"Gordon, have you ever been in love?"

"No, I haven't," he said. He took a draw from a water bottle I held out. "I've liked people a whole lot, but not love."

"You're not in love with Brenda?"

"No. What is this all about?"

I rode as slowly as he ran, making myself balance on the skinny tires.

"I've met someone," I said. "I can't say where. I think I've found my soul mate."

"What is she like?"

"She's exceptional. She has it all. Brains, music, athletic ability. She's a swimmer and she plays clarinet. And she makes me laugh." The twin lighthouses of Makepeace Island emerged as we turned a bend. I thought how great it was that they had stood so long together.

"Is she pretty?" Gordy asked.

"She's amazing. In every way imaginable."

Gordy smiled and bumped my fist. "I knew she would be," he said.

all-state

Looking at all this information," Gordy asked, "what do you think is most interesting?"

We were in Gordy's living room, which had dark green walls, a grandfather clock, and glass-fronted bookcases filled with old books. Through the open windows came the fresh, cool smell of salt water and the begging of gulls that followed lobster boats. We had printed a lot of info off the Internet as a starting point, then highlighted some pages and laid them out on the coffee table.

"The two things that jump out at me are that the harmonica was invented by a sixteen-year-old and that in some countries it's called a mouth organ. But I wouldn't necessarily want to say 'mouth organ' in front of Shelley Dietrich or Dani Solomon. Or Brenda." If I said anything remotely sexual, I turned bright red, in a way that probably revealed that I had never had a girlfriend.

Gordy circled some notes with a red marker. "What else?"

"That the harmonica is being used as therapy for people with respiratory problems. And that Abraham Lincoln carried one in his pocket."

"What music do you want to use?"

From Gordy's CDs on the table I picked out *Harmonica Masters: Classic Recordings from the 1920s and 1930s.*

Gordy started the disc in the player above the bookcase. "Let's start pulling it together. Why don't you make up an outline?"

"You outline your papers?"

"Usually."

"Do you ever get tired of being so perfect?"

"I'm not perfect."

"My dad thinks you and I should start a band."

"That's not a bad idea. I can play lead. Who would we get for the drummer and bass player?"

"I have no interest in starting a band. I don't consider myself a musician anymore. I've decided that my real strength is helping people. I'm a helper first and a musician second."

On the opposite wall from where I was sitting were two large oil paintings. One showed a bare tree from across a salt marsh, the other a grove of straight, identical trees with falling leaves. I didn't know much about art, but I thought the paintings were between abstract and realistic. And that these seemed to have a personality or vision or uniqueness without being actually weird.

"My dad knows that artist from Maine," Gordy said. "She lives on Little Cranberry Island, and we've visited her a couple of times."

"I love those," I said. "I wish Dad could paint like that."

"How is the show going?"

"Not well. Maybe my dad would be better off if he hadn't lost touch with his art school friends. If he had some other painters to bounce things off of. Sort of like me with you and this paper."

"Someone whose opinion he trusted," Gordy said.

"My mom thinks Dad might be an unrecognized genius." I stared at Gordy until he got the idea. "Not likely."

"So you're still worried about him?" Gordon asked.

"More every day. My mom and Linda are acting sort of nuts too. If I didn't have Listeners to go to, I'd probably be nuts myself." And Jenney. I'd be nuts without Jenney.

"Should we get to work?" Gordy asked, picking up the music history research.

I took the papers from him and put them in my pack. "No, I need to go. It's only four o'clock. I want to go into his studio and see what he's working on. If I rush, I'll have enough time to get in and out before Dad gets home."

I rode home, past the stone wall and twisted trees of Beauport Beach, the copper-colored granite ledges, and the wall inscribed with the names of fishermen lost at sea. My legs and my mind worked equally hard—one fed the other.

A solution. Something to do. It's good to do something. It's torture to do nothing when there's something you can do.

67.

last winter: the sharp objects

We've spent three months taking care of Dad at home. We've tried fish oil, calisthenics, sunlight, and affirmations. Meditation, vitamin B, and aromatherapy. But Dad has gotten worse instead of better. He says that we don't really care about him, that we are just pretending. He says "I'm so tired" and "It's the beginning of the end." From the little he says, I believe he's thinking of killing himself.

Linda, Jodie, and I form a suicide-prevention team. Without disturbing Dad, we move from room to room collecting all the sharp objects: razors, scissors, Grandpa Eddie's fishing knife. We drop them in a metal box that we plan to hide in this very room, in the crawl space above what is now Dad's studio.

Mom comes home and finds me in the kitchen, testing the edges of the carrot peeler and the cheese slicer.

"What are you doing?" she asks.

I'm the oldest, so I should explain. "We're hiding the sharp objects so Dad can't kill himself." Linda and Jodie are brave. They don't cry or hold on to each other, so neither do I.

Mom finds Dad sitting in front of the TV. She says his name over and over, even though he says nothing back.

She comes back to the kitchen and takes her phone out of her purse. She calls the therapist we rejected months ago and says Dad needs to start seeing him again.

Everything we tried has been a failure.

68.

catalogue

I threw Triumph on the front lawn, her front wheel still spinning. No cars. No Linda—she must be at Jodie's. I went into Dad's "studio." I locked the outside door and wedged a paint-spattered stool under the knob of the door leading into the house. Still sweating from the ride, I spun around and came face-to-face with my father's insanity. I imagined the reporters and the TV teams and the gallery and museum people. All of them armed with cameras. All eager to show the world the contents of this room.

The fruit with faces. *Click.*

The skydiving fish. *Click.*

The marauding tree. *Click.*

The perverted sunsets. *Click, click.*

And I found more. A Child and Madonna with a huge Baby Jesus holding a tiny Mary. A toilet that doubled as an electric chair. A giant fetus with Dad's face. A dollar bill with George Washington as a transvestite. An aerial view of a platoon of soldiers carrying a casket. The flag on the casket said DON'T ASK, DON'T KILL.

No one would understand. No one would get what he was saying. Everyone would know what we tried so long to hide. Everyone would know.

PART 3

freckled

Goddamn it, Jodie! If you don't know what you're doing, why do you even pick up the tools?" I heard the commotion and raced from my room toward Dad's studio.

In the studio, Dad grabbed a hammer and a frame from Jodie's hands. He threw them in her direction, and they clattered to the floor. Beside her, a box of tacks toppled off the old kitchen table and spilled around her feet.

Jodie's eyes got as big as the eyes on Dad's fetus painting. She gasped and held her breath. She was afraid of either breaking something or having something else thrown at her.

Linda leaped between Jodie and Dad. "Don't talk to her like that!"

I rushed to Dad and stopped his arm. "You're gonna hurt somebody!" I whispered, "That was out of line, Dad."

I had to give Jodie credit. It took her a full minute to start crying. At first her face got red and she looked like she smelled a bad smell. But she looked Dad right in the eye.

"I was only trying to help," she said. Dad should have apologized right there, but he just kicked the loose tacks into a corner so no one would step on them.

"Well," he said, "why don't we get back to work?"

"I should go home," Jodie told Linda. She walked out of the studio with her shoulders shaking.

Jodie called her mother from the wall phone in our kitchen, asking to be picked up. Her mother asked some question on the other end, and Jodie said, "I'll tell you later."

As Jodie stood by the front door, her bangs stuck to her face and her nose ran. I heard gray, mouselike hiccups. I got a paper towel for her nose.

Linda had stayed behind with Dad. Once Jodie's mom picked her up, I went back to the studio.

"How could you do that?" Linda demanded. "Now she won't want to come back!" Her voice was wild, like something was being torn from her.

Dad's voice was eerily calm as he picked up the thrown items. "The specific personnel is not important, Linda-Lou. The work itself is what's important."

"But it was good before when all of us worked together." She tore off her beret and hung it on a hook by the door.

"You should be honored to be chosen for a project like this," Dad said. "It may be the greatest honor you ever receive."

Linda and I looked at each other. I knew we were both thinking the same thing: that whatever had been happening for the past several weeks was about to come to an end.

lost horizon

How much more proof do you need, Mom?" I thrust the NIMH printout under her face as soon as she got home from work. "He's jumpy and wired, he's talking too fast, he hardly sleeps, he spends too much money, he thinks he has genius-level abilities, he's taken on an impossible new project. . . . He could be the poster boy. He has nearly every symptom!"

"That man is not Dad," Linda said, pointing toward the studio. Her voice had been breaking in ragged bursts since Jodie's departure. "Give me Dad back."

"I don't know," Mom said. She waved away my list from the website. She stalked around the room, peering through the curtains at the street, moving throw pillows, straightening magazines. I could see how hard this was for her to accept. She had been glad Dad was busy. She had been working all the time herself. She was one of the people who believed that high productivity was a sign of, if not mental health, then something else really good that there was no name for.

"All right," she said. She took a few steps in that direction, then came back to us. "I'll talk to him. Not tonight. Tomorrow morning, when he's had some rest. And if I have to talk to Dr. Fritz and Dr. Gupta, I'll do that, too."

"And you have to call off the art show," I said.

Mom moved back to the window. She looked outside like someone with stage fright checking out the audience. "I'm not ready to do that yet," she said. "I'll talk to the doctors about it. I'll tell them everything you said."

I went up close behind Mom. "You remind me of Dad right now," I told her. "The way he used to walk around as if he was looking for something."

"I am looking for something," Mom said. "I'm looking for a dream your father and I had and we lost and I thought we had found again. I guess I'm having trouble accepting that what we had wasn't real."

last winter: treatment

Mr. Misuraca, my history teacher from last year, moves up and down the rows, handing out a quiz. He moves hulkingly, like a circus bear trained to stand on his hind legs. Brenda Mason is here, stroking the soft mohair of her sweater sleeve while she starts filling in her quiz. I write my name, but nothing more.

Mom and Uncle Marty are taking Dad to the hospital for his first treatment. She tells me the plan in detail, so I'll know where they are every minute. The traffic is light on Route 128 so early in the morning but grows heavier on Route 1. The car stops at the Dunkin Donuts on Route 1. Then it continues past the Christmas Tree Shop and the Salvation Army and the minigolf course with the dinosaur. Soon Mom and Marty see buildings of the Boston skyline, jagged and official, stalagmites in a cave they won't be able to get out of.

They continue onto Storrow Drive and along the Charles River to the Longwood Medical Area. Uncle

Marty drops off Mom and Dad at Building G and parks the car on the fourth floor of the Coolidge Hospital garage.

Mom takes Dad to the basement and helps him sign in with the receptionist. Dad is wearing a new sweater and a pair of my pants. A nurse calls Dad's name and walks him through a set of swinging doors. He meets a doctor he's never seen before.

The doctor has Dad lie on a cot with restraints. A nurse straps him down and injects him with muscle relaxant. Once all the muscles in Dad's body have let go, the nurse rubs something like Vaseline on Dad's head and fits an oxygen mask over Dad's face. The doctor attaches a wire with two contacts to Dad's forehead. Dad appears to be sleeping, and the doctor pulls a lever like a giant light switch.

I stare at my history quiz while an electric current is sent through my father's body. This must never happen again.

last winter: puzzle

Dad sits beside me on the couch the day after his first shock treatment. He wants to know when his mother is coming to get him. His mother has been dead for ten years. I distract him by starting a crossword puzzle, but he doesn't know how to spell "knee." He is wearing my pants. I am wearing my pants. I don't know where he ends and I begin. This must never happen again.

shift 8, november 29. call 57

Listeners. Can I help you?"

It's me.

"Thank God you called, Jenney. There's nobody here. I really need to talk to you."

You're not going to believe what happened.

"My dad totally lost it today. He really is manic. He started yelling at my sister's friend."

Oh, no, Billy. That's awful.

"He's had a total personality change. He used to be this funny, cool, low-key guy, and now he's turned into an egomaniac no one can stand. At least, I can't stand. He has this idea that he's a tremendous painter. He's inviting all these museum and media people to this art show that he's having on December fourth, and it's going to be an absolute fiasco."

Are you sure?

"Yes. Because his work is really bad. Like, embarrassingly bad."

That must make you so sad. Does your mom know about this? What does she think?

"My mom doesn't entirely accept a realistic interpretation of what's going on. She's in it with him, like a mutual delusion. I'm just dreading it. Every day that goes by brings me closer to being humiliated."

Why do you have to be humiliated? I told you before. You're not the one who's a bad artist.

"You're right. But I hate the idea of even being there. I should make a point of being far, far away. Listen, what's going on with you? You sound really anxious."

I'm in a state of panic. It's been the worst day. I wish I hadn't even gotten out of bed this morning.

"You had a crappy day too?"

Crappy doesn't begin to describe it.

"Take a deep breath. What's going on?"

My parents.

"Oh, no. What are they trying to pull this time?"

It was awful. And I feel bad but I don't, because I think it was my fault. Wait. That didn't make sense.

"They contacted you?"

They sent me a letter. And then my mom called.

"What did she want?"

They're doing it. They're taking action against Melinda. Just like they threatened to.

"No! What reason could they possibly have?"

We had another argument about it. They said they're giving me one more chance to stop treatment with her and take back the accusations, and if I don't, they're going to sue Melinda and have her license taken away.

"They would really do that?"

How can they blame me? They're the ones who ruined our relationship. They're the ones who couldn't be trusted. I didn't ask to remember these things.

"Did they say they blamed you?"

Sorry, I can hardly talk. It's too much sometimes. Sometimes the feelings are overwhelming. The soft clicking noise returned.

"Don't worry. Your parents can't defeat you, not on your good days. You're going to do fine."

I am not going to worry about them. I am not going to protect them. I can only worry about myself. I need to cut all ties with my parents. That's all I can do at this point if I want to keep my sanity.

"My mom's that way too. It's like she's blind with anything that has to do with my dad. She wants to believe I'm the one who's wrong. Jenney, are you feeling suicidal?"

No. Just hopeless. Billy, are you feeling suicidal?

"No. Just completely demoralized."

That was a joke. Not a very good one, I admit. Look, I should go. I would talk longer, but I want to check in with Melinda again before I go to bed. She said if I could catch her before eleven, we could talk about what to do next. I wonder if there's some way I can go before a judge and tell him how great Melinda has been to me. How much she's helped me.

"Can we talk again soon? Things at my house will probably keep getting worse."

Save some time for me on your next shift. I want to know everything that's going on. For now you hang in, all right? Be strong for me.

"You remember what an incredible person you are. You don't have to feel sorry about anything you've done. Remember that, okay?"

I will. Let's check in soon, Hallmark.

I had looked forward to this call all day. The fact that it was so short was the worst event of the day, worse than Dad acting sicker, worse than Mom not acknowledging how bad he was. But I had to be strong, like Jenney was strong. As long as I had Jenney, I would survive.

74.

original

First thing the next morning I texted Gordon: "Can you meet me before my first class? I need you to do something for me."

"Sure," he sent back. "Anything."

We met outside my homeroom and started walking. I stopped in front of the health bulletin board and looked up and down the hall.

"Can you and your dad come to the show a little early and he can let me know what he thinks?" I asked. "Then, if the paintings are as crazy as I think they are, I'm going to shut the place down and ask everyone to leave."

Gordy pressed his lips together and glanced to one side. He looked like someone at a dinner table who has begun to chew something bad and is deciding how to secretly get rid of it.

"Is that really what you want?" he asked.

"I think it's the most sensible course of action."

"I would never want to hurt his feelings unless it was a

real emergency. How would your dad feel if you did what you said you were going to do? Shut down his art show?"

"He would probably be ticked off, but I hope he would thank me later."

"All right, then. I'll bring my dad early. But I won't prepare him at all. We'll just see what he says."

We cut through the courtyard. A few girls ogled Gordon in his aquamarine dress shirt. He didn't realize it. He was sort of a hidden gem where girls were concerned. None of them ogled me, because they didn't like the bouncing.

"Have you written your essay?" Gordy asked.

"I can't worry about that now. I've got too much on my mind."

"Have you done anything with it at all?"

"I'll work on it tonight. As soon as I get out of Listeners."

"Brenda and I might see *Real Steel*. Andy said it's the best movie ever made."

"Can I ask you something?" I angled my head to beckon him closer. "How do you know you're not in love with Brenda?"

Gordy looked around and hesitated. "If you're in love with someone, every time you see her you feel like you're going to pass out. And you get this little thrill like, 'Oooh, there she is.'"

"She's in love with you, though."

"I think so. I feel sort of dishonest about that. About letting it go on. So, when are you going to introduce me to your girlfriend?"

"It's too early," I said. "The whole situation is kind of delicate."

After class I had a free study period. I went into the library, opened one of my notebooks, and made a list.

top ten reasons i love jenney

10. Loyal friend. Stac. and Reb. blow her off but Jen. always forgives/forgets, tries again.
9. Ambitious. Coll. plan falls into dung heap. She makes new plan.
8. Resilient. Horrib. parents can't keep her down.
7. Generous & compassionate. Wants to give, not just take. Wants to be Listener. Even now when think about that, nose gets tingly.
6. Funny. Big Ear, etc.
5. Achievements. Academics, swimming. Is somebody.
4. She's beautiful.
3. Thinks I'm special! Thinks I'm best one. Picked me out of crowd.
2. I understand her.
1. She understands me.

I underlined her name and raised the paper as if I were holding a portrait in a frame. My list captured Jenney perfectly. I couldn't wait to introduce her to Gordon. I couldn't wait to meet her myself. I wanted her to be with me on Sunday. She was the only one who could help me through it. She would get me through the crisis, just like I was getting her through hers. I would be embarrassed about Dad's art, but we could ignore it and make a joke of it. The show would make a crazy backdrop for our first day together. Maybe technically our meeting was too soon because I was a Listener and she was a caller, but since she was planning to volunteer once she got back on her feet, we would meet in the office at some point anyway.

In the library I watched some senior couples doing their homework together. They used to seem mature to me. But I was more mature than they were. They had met each other in school, and I had met Jenney in the real world.

shift 9, december 2. call 42

"Listeners. Can I help you?"

It's me.

"Jenney? What's wrong?"

Are you on by yourself?

"Yeah. We can talk. What is it?"

I had a really bad session with Melinda.

"I'm sorry."

She terminated my therapy.

"What do you mean?"

She said she can't work with me anymore.

The soft sound like clicking began, then grew. It shifted from Jenney's throat to lower in her body and from a cat's paws to a steady pounding of footsteps.

"Why would she say that?"

She said my parents' lawyer had sent her a letter, a cease-and-desist order demanding that she stop treating me. And so she has to, by law. She said she would be committing professional suicide to keep seeing me. She could even be put in jail, locked up. Or at least sued and have her license taken away.

"That's terrible. You really rely on Melinda."

I do. She's helped me so much. She's helped me to see them for who they are.

"What will you do now?"

She said she hoped I would at least try to get another therapist because she didn't want to leave me high and dry. She gave . . .

"Go on."

She gave me a list of other therapists I might call, but she told me that there was a good chance none of them would work with me once word got out about my parents threatening to sue. She said there was a chance that I wouldn't be able to find another therapist unless I went to someone my parents picked out for me.

"Do you want to do that?"

No! Of course not! Why would I go to someone who's in my parents' pocket? Someone who would probably tell them everything I said. My God. They really have me where they want me now. I'm completely trapped. I can't believe I lost Melinda. I'm all alone.

"You're not alone. How can you say that?"

I am alone. You have no idea. What Melinda and I were working on, dredging up all the stuff from the past. You can't really do it alone. You need someone to help you. Now Melinda is gone. All of a sudden. I'm—in shock.

"You're not alone, Jenney. You have me."

I know I do, but—

"You have me, and I'll always stand beside you, no

matter what. We'll aways have each other. As long as we have each other, we can make it."

Thank you. At least I know someone's in my corner.

"So what will you do about getting a therapist?"

I don't know. I'm . . . cornered. That's the thing about powerful people. They hold all the cards. They can make stuff happen. Or not happen. Will you hold on? I need to get a glass of water.

"Sure."

So, how are you?

"Not much better than you are. It's a bad day on this end, too."

What's happening with the art show? It's this weekend, right?

"Sunday. Jenney, will you come to the show?"

Do you mean it? Are you serious?

"If you're there with me, I'll be all right. I'd love to meet you in person anyway. What do you think?"

I don't know.

"Please come. It's the only way I can get through it."

I'm flattered. That nose-huffing noise started again. It didn't sound gross. It sounded delicate.

"Are you crying?"

No, I'm laughing. I've never met a Listener in person.

"Well, you and I are different. We're real friends now. Come on, it could be fun."

Where do you live?

"At 32 Ithaca Street, up behind the highway. Do you know the Italian bakery? We're right near there. The first house after the mailbox. We have a white rock at the end of the driveway, and a bright orange door."

I've been so tired since Melinda told me. Every bone in my body is worn out. All I want to do is pull the covers over my head and sleep. I can't say for sure. But I'll try. What time?

"All day, from ten to four. What time can you get there?"

I said I would try. Hey, how will we recognize each other?

"You'll recognize me because I'll be living there."

You'll recognize me because I'm—

"No, don't tell me."

You don't want to know what I look like?

"I want to be surprised."

What if I'm ugly?

"You could never be ugly to me."

All right, well, I'm going to try to sleep for a while. Maybe I'll see you Sunday if we don't talk again first.

"Sleep well, and try not to worry. And, Jenney—thanks."

For what?

"For listening."

Good night, Hallmark.

racing

After closing up at Listeners I took an hour-long ride in the cold fall air. Past all the downtown stores with their Christmas cutouts on the doors. Out from the town center and along the waterfront. Up to Portuguese Hill, where mechanical deer assembled on lawns, bowing creakily under strings of white lights. I stood on a ledge of granite and looked out over the harbor. A massive industrial fishing boat worked its way to Georges Bank through the almost empty waters. Nothing around me but space and stars and cold, cold air. Like Hagrid, I could think about jumping. But instead I thought about how powerful it was to be alone. Not beholden to anyone. Jenney was right. When the art show began, I could choose not to be humiliated.

My legs felt warm and loose after the ride, but when I saw the light in Dad's studio my body tensed again. I carried Triumph to my room. It was not until morning that I realized I'd let another week pass without writing my paper.

PART 4

7 8.

whether

Saturday, December 3. I hovered outside the den while
my family watched the weather reports. Uncle Marty, who
had a weather radio, was calling Dad with updates every
half hour.

"What's wrong with people?" Mom complained. "It's
New England, it's winter, and it's cold. Does that mean
they have to stay in all day?"

Dad flipped the channel. "The TV stations have to
make a big deal out of it. That's how they get their adver-
tising dollars."

"I can't believe that guy said 'brrr,'" said Linda. "It's
such a cliché."

"It won't be that bad," Jodie added. "*The Old Farmer's
Almanac* says flurries, then sunny and cold. I checked it
three weeks ago." Jodie had forgiven my father after he
went to her house, alone, to apologize to both her and her
parents.

"I don't know about the *Almanac*." Mom said. "I don't

216

see how anyone can predict an entire year's weather in advance."

"I don't either. But my mom says they're usually right. She uses it to plan all our vacations."

Jodie's vacations were a sore spot for Mom. Once, her family flew first class to Palm Beach, Florida, and invited Linda along. Jodie's mother took both girls for spray-on tans without asking Mom. That was when Linda first began staring at herself in the mirror and calling herself "Lucky Linda." Mom told her she shouldn't be obsessed with her appearance.

"Pretty rules one, Linda," she said at the time. "Smart rules the world." But I think the real problem was that the trip was expensive and Mom and Dad could never duplicate it.

Mom grabbed the remote from Dad. She surfed for another opinion on the weather.

All of them were in for a shock tomorrow, when I brought a girl home for the first time. Mom would like Jenney's manners and smarts. Linda and Jodie might tease me. But Jenney would see how I lived. For better or for worse. How much I had to put up with.

suspended

At one thirty in the morning, Dad was still up. Mom was asleep—no sound there—and Jodie and Linda were snuggled in one bed under the watchful eye of Linda's Garfield. It was a special night for those two: Linda lent Jodie a nightshirt of our grandma's with a disco scene on the front, and Jodie asked if she could keep it, and Linda said yes. They would probably both write about it in their diary.

"Okay, Dad," I said, "let's bring it on home." At least he was in pajamas, not paint-spattered clothes. "It's a lot of stress, Dad."

"Almost done, Billy, almost done. I got an idea for suspending some of the work with fishing line." He sat beside the living room coffee table, where he was cutting the line into equal lengths with a pocketknife.

Dad looked so dedicated. Maybe I should make an effort, I thought, by doing some last-minute chore for the show.

"Do you want help with anything?"

"Yes. Would you do me a favor?"

"Sure." I sat on the couch, ready to help with cutting.

He put the knife down and rested his hand on mine. "When you become a dad, don't be staid and predictable. Surprise them once in a while, okay? Be the kind of guy who keeps a surprise up his sleeve."

watchful

Dad ate a sandwich and went to bed. Maybe he fell asleep like the other three, but now I was wide awake. I kept thinking about the weather and about how the show would probably be ruined, and how Dad might have to have shock treatments again or be hospitalized or spend his life looping crazily from lows to highs. I couldn't relax. I felt tight and inanimate, like a surfboard laid on a roof rack. But then Jenney's voice crept into my mind.

Tough day, Hallmark?

I wiggled my toes, and my shoulders and back melted into the pillows.

dawn

As I dressed for an early bike ride, bare tree branches waved in my window, and a few brown leaves blew across the street in parallel lines. No snow yet.

Outside, the frozen grass crunched under my feet like cereal. I mounted my bike and rolled down the hill. The houses had a feeling of sleep, or if not sleep, waiting. A mile out, the inns and hotels across from the beach were shuttered for the winter. The damp beach looked useless and insipid. There seemed to be no point to its being there when people weren't using it. But that was our perspective, not the beach's.

I leaned my bike against the boulevard railing and stepped down. The ocean, sometimes so fearsome, was a puddle today. The half-inch waves struck the shore like a glass of water spilled across a tablecloth. I picked up three large rocks and tossed them into the deepest water I could reach, and each made its own mushroom cloud. A few yards out, black-and-white shorebirds sat one per boulder, each sure his boulder was the best and the most important. Everything I saw was more vivid than usual. I had a feeling of before and after, of a decision being made. When Jenney met me, I wondered, would she be disappointed?

Near the beach was the tennis court where Dad had tried to interest me in the game. When I was eleven I thought I had gotten as good as Dad, until I watched him play with his friends and saw how he really served.

The sky held back the snow in a big curve, like a hammock holding a body. One person was out jogging. She wore an iPod and a T-shirt that said ARMY. Her breath made a cumulus in the cold air, and her face shone holiday red. But when I said hello she glared as if I shouldn't be here. When you were a guy alone, girls glared at you.

I pictured Jenney riding a Raleigh, and pretty fast too. Soon I wouldn't be alone. Jenney and I would take the bus, or her car—she had a car—to western Mass., to the Berkshires, and do a century in the mountains. That was a hundred miles in one day.

I sat on a bench as the snow began to fall. The sky released its weight in tiny fragments like skin cells. After a while I rolled down the walking path on a sheet of white unmarked by footprints or paw prints. My bike drew a solid line one and a half inches wide. Unlike the foot and paw prints, my track let no one guess how large I was.

In a gazebo above the cliffs, I unwrapped a sleeve of Fig Newtons for my breakfast. The punctuation-size seeds resisted my teeth. Beyond the cliffs was Havenswood, a forest where I often rode the trails. The path was dry there because the snow got caught up in the trees. I gave it my all for twenty minutes. My speed blurred automotively the house foundations and stone walls that marked property lines no longer recognized. I came to a destination: more a point in time than a point of place. I didn't have my watch or phone, but in my heart I knew it was nine o'clock. In one hour she could be at the house. I stored up breath and turned Triumph around. Like the day I sat with my hand on the phone receiver and dedicated my service to my close family member, I had no idea what was about to happen.

the inevitable

As Triumph climbed the hill to my house, the sky was flat and gray. Aside from one of Dad's posters taped to the mailbox with a bunch of silver balloons, the house looked normal, the way it did when it housed the five of us and no outsiders. Unassuming, predictable, and safe. Hard to believe that in twenty minutes, people—including museum people and reporters and Jenney—would or would not arrive, and Dad would or would not make a fool of himself. The sky was as gray as tin, but the snow was slowing, and I would have liked to paint this feeling as I stood in the road and counted the last five flakes falling on the asphalt around my feet. I waited to see if they would stay frozen or dissolve. When they melted, I took it as a sign that the day was getting warmer. A good sign.

83.

separate

I carried Triumph through the vacuumed, dusted, and plumped living room. The show was out in the garage, but Mom and Dad must have cleaned inside for people who needed the bathroom. I wondered if Jenney would come inside and whether, being rich, she would think our house was nice. Yesterday I had picked out my jeans, shirt, and sweater. I never really ironed, but I folded and stacked the clothes so they would be smooth. Now I took a shower and washed my helmet-felted hair, checked my shirt buttons to give Jenney the impression that I noticed what I looked like. I went to the back of the house and stood inside the screen door one last time.

I stepped into the garage and saw artwork hung at every level along the splintery walls and on the posts, resting on tables arranged in a square, and on temporary dividers made of plywood. In the center several small marine paintings hung from fishing line, as if they were floating. My family was too busy to notice me. In the left corner,

Jodie arranged some notebooks and a vase of flowers on a card table. Dad took one more look around the room. He must not have slept, because his eyes were creased. He clenched his hands as if he were praying. Mom and Linda held tight to Dad on either side. All at once the four of them looked in the same direction—toward the gate that joined the driveway to the yard. Dad unlinked himself and stepped forward.

one-man show

True to Gordy's word, he and his dad were the first guests. Gordy half-hugged, half-choked me and gave Mom a box of fancy cookies that she put on the refreshment table. Donald Abt wore a leather jacket and motorcycle boots. Although he was a lawyer, he looked hip because he hung out with musicians.

"Pretty exciting, Bill," he said. "You've waited a long time for this day, I hear."

The doorbell rang, and Dad's friend June arrived with two of his coworkers. She carried a bunch of white helium balloons printed with the phrase WOO-HOO!

"Not a very intellectual message, I'm afraid," she said, "but they express how I feel."

"Me too," said Dad. Linda tied June's balloons to the mailbox with the other bunch. Gordon, Donald, and Dad's office friends walked along the back wall. They stopped at the fruit-bowl series.

In the center work—titled *Where Does It Come*

From?—each piece of fruit had a migrant worker's face. Dad tried to capture in a few strokes the fatigue and tenacity of some workers in a *New York Times* profile he'd taped on the studio wall as a reference. The worker-fruits wore straw hats or baseball caps, and an entire bunch of grapes had kids' faces.

"Wow," Donald Abt said. "I feel that like a punch in the gut." Gordy widened his eyes at me.

People from Mom's museum showed up next. "The light at the top of your hill is remarkable," Mom's volunteer docent, Mrs. Armenian, commented. "Even on a gray day, it's so—"

"Luminous?" Mom suggested.

"Yes, luminous. And the gray sky coming through the windows makes the colors in your husband's paintings just *pop*."

June zeroed in on the killer-tree painting. In white pants and a white parka with fur around the hood, she looked like a monarch in a Hans Christian Andersen story. Having been through last winter with us, she was probably worried like I was. I'm pretty sure she would have bought something whether Dad's work was good or bad, but having seen something she wanted to own, she looked relieved and happy. I admired June even more.

"It was a wonderful fall, wasn't it?" she asked me, laughing at the tourist-eating tree.

"It was a *really* wonderful fall," I told her, thinking about my secret. I checked the door to see if Jenney had shown up yet. She and June would really hit it off. My mouth got so dry that I couldn't close my lips after talking or smiling. My head felt groggy and I wanted to nap. To avoid the rest of the day and to wake up when it was tomorrow.

Mom's former boss, Pudge, arrived next with his husband, Kenneth. They gravitated toward the sunsets.

"Ruthless," Kenneth said. "The way he subverts the clichés."

Pudge spotted my sister wearing a velvet suit of Grandma Pearl's with a partridge on the shoulder. "Linda— so elegant and grown up. I barely recognized you."

Jodie offered Pudge and Kenneth hot cocoa from a tray. She and Linda had spent hours deciding on Styrofoam or real mugs. To underscore Dad's environmental concerns, they decided to buy mugs at the dollar store and donate them to a homeless shelter after the show. Linda wanted to charge for the cocoa, but Jodie convinced her it should be free.

"You've thought of everything," Pudge said.

"Is your coat real cashmere?" Linda asked Kenneth.

"It is."

Linda saw me watching them. "See, Billy? It's not wrong to have money and nice things."

"As long as you remember there are some things money can't buy," added Jodie.

"That's a cliché that should never be subverted," Pudge agreed.

"Is that John Cage?" Mr. Abt asked. A phrase from the CD drowned under the highway noise.

"That's right," Linda said. "Dad wanted to go a little edgy with the music. Should I turn it up?"

I saw Gordy's dad talking to Uncle Marty. They were both holding the notebooks Jodie had laid out on the table. The books identified the paintings by location and title, their size, and the medium (mostly oil). The first page had a photo of Dad along with his artist's statement, giving his biography and telling how he got the ideas for the show. The cover said ALL PAINTINGS PRICED REASON-ABLY. I saw Linda's hand in that.

"I'm so proud," Uncle Marty was telling Mr. Abt.

"Your father is a really good painter," Mr. Abt said to me. He got out his cell phone. "Do you mind? I'm going to make sure my law partner sees these. But he'll probably say your dad didn't set his prices high enough."

My chest opened partway, and my head felt as light and empty as one of June's balloons. I couldn't believe Mr. Abt thought Dad's paintings were good. Many times I pictured Jenney helping me through my misery. I hadn't imagined her sharing my pride.

"It's not about the money," I said. "Glad you're enjoying yourself, Mr. Abt."

"I'm planning to buy one," Marty told me. "I want a Bill Morrison to hang up in the bar. The one I want is pretty steep, but I don't want bro giving me any discounts. I suppose you know which one it is."

He smiled like I was expected to know something.

"I have no idea what you're talking about," I told Marty.

"Come on, Billy, you're being cute with me." He turned up the collar of his wool blazer against the cold. The electric heaters Linda had plugged in weren't warming the space yet. "I want the painting of you."

Dr. Fritz arrived. He had lots of degrees but dressed like a lumberjack. With him was a woman with long gray hair. "Billy, this is my wife, Geraldine Perkins. She's a painter too."

Geraldine gravitated toward the wharf miniatures.

"These are our small paintings," Linda told her.

"Very strong," Geraldine commented to her husband about a decrepit fishing boat.

"I'm not surprised," he said. "Not surprised in the least."

Jodie interrupted Dad to introduce him to a stranger. It was a reporter from the *Hawthorne Beacon-Times* asking to photograph Dad and have him write a "My View" column on the state of painting.

In the right corner of the garage Mom's Brooksbie friends clustered in front of a large vertical painting.

"Exquisite draftsmanship," one woman said. "Almost photorealistic." I recognized her as the painter of the malicious chicken that hung in our dining room.

Dad's painting was maybe three feet by five and made up of about three hundred small gray blocks on a grid. I could barely make out the subject until I stood back. I saw a close, cut-off version of my own face. My eyes were narrowed and my mouth was thin and stiff. My fingertips pressed against the screen so tightly that they flattened into discs, like the fingertips of a tree frog. The crowd of Brooksbie people parted, waiting for me to speak.

I hadn't even known he was looking at me.

watching dad

By one o'clock I hadn't seen Jenney, but I had gotten used to my portrait. I planned to get her some cocoa and take her by the arm and walk her to that painting first. That way when she met my parents she would have something to talk to them about.

At 1:10 Pudge told Dad that the Museum of New England Heritage didn't have funds right now for new acquisitions, but he asked if Dad would lend *Where Does It Come From?* indefinitely, to be hung in the lounge area near the vending machines.

"Right now, unfortunately, it's a thought-free zone," Pudge told him.

"Why don't we talk?" Dad replied.

she?

At one fifteen a girl in a long down coat, with a ski hat covering honey-colored curls, walked up the driveway. I stood by our mailbox as if my legs were two more posts driven into the concrete.

"Is this where the art show is?" she asked.

"It absolutely is," I said. "Welcome to 32 Ithaca Street."

"You must be the son of the artist."

"That's right, I'm Billy," I said. I took her mittened hand in both of mine. She was beautiful. Not perfect, but strong and full of life. Someone who turned every hurt and insult into fuel for an opportunity. Every kick is a boost, as Mom said. I wondered if I should hug her or wait for her to hug me.

She squeezed my arm. "I've heard so much about you. I'm Tish London. I work with your mom at the museum."

I felt my smile fade. "Let me take you to see Mom." I walked Tish to the garage and then came back to my sentry post at the end of the driveway.

"Who was that?" Gordy asked a minute later, bringing me cocoa in an ATLANTIC CITY NEW JERSEY mug.

"A coworker of my Mom's."

"Pretty."

"She's okay." I watched the lower half of our road, the direction where people would likely come from downtown. I had never asked Jenney what type of car she drove.

"The way you reacted, I thought she was special for some reason."

"Well, no."

"You seem on edge."

"I'm planning to meet someone here. That girl you saw, I thought she was the one I'm going to meet."

"You don't know what she looks like?"

"Not really."

Gordon raised his eyebrows. This was the second time he had asked about Jenney's looks.

"How do you know her, from a chat room or something?"

"No. All right, Gordy." Deep breath. "Can you keep a secret?"

"Of course I can."

"Because no way can anyone find out about this." I spoke to him with half my attention, while keeping an eye on the people who arrived.

I leaned in and tapped his parka sleeve with my index finger. "I'm sort of involved with somebody at Listeners."

Gordy rocked back and forth in the cold. "One of the volunteers? Cool. Why didn't you tell me?"

"No, one of the callers."

His mouth opened and he closed it again. "Oh, is that allowed?" he finally said.

"No, it absolutely is not allowed. It would get me kicked out of there." I shook my head and laughed over my cup like a worn-out guy sitting at a bar, implying that although my relationship with Jenney was against the rules, it was "just one of those things."

"Why are you doing it, then?"

I climbed onto the white rock Linda had painted. Jenney would see the rock, 32 MORRISON, and me.

"Because . . . How can I put this? Because I've never felt such a connection with any girl before. What's happening with this girl and me . . . well, it's going to have a happy ending. This first part where I'm breaking a rule is the only weird part. And the first part will end up meaning nothing in the long run. In the story of who we'll be together."

People waved as they flowed in and out of the yard, but no one interrupted our conversation. The garage was where the action was. Gordon looked around for his dad. Donald Abt was still inside the garage, talking to June Melman, and showed no signs of leaving.

"Not that I know anything about this," Gordon continued, "but what you're doing sounds really sketchy. If I worked at a suicide hotline, I'd want to follow all the rules. People's lives are at stake, right?"

My face got hot. Because he didn't know Jenney. "Jenney isn't one of those people. She's the smartest girl I know. She gives great advice. She's had problems in life, definitely, but she's got both feet on the ground. She could be a volunteer herself." I smiled, remembering my promise to give her a cushion.

"So this must be the girl you asked me about on my run that day. The amazing one."

"It is." I teetered on the rock as if it was a skateboard. I started to fall, and Gordon grabbed my arm.

"That's why you couldn't say more. Because of the hotline."

"Right," I said. "Now you know everything." The conversation had that wrapping-up-discoveries feeling, like the end of a Sherlock Holmes movie.

"Wow. It seems like you think a lot of her."

"She's unbelievable, Gord. I can't wait for you to meet her."

"But the hotline thing is definitely an obstacle." Gordon pulled me off the rock. I had the feeling he was about to drag me inside.

"It doesn't have to be. Lots of couples have gotten over obstacles in order to be together."

"It does have to be," Gordon said.

"Why?" Another photographer, and someone with a video camera, arrived, and I pointed them toward the garage. I got the impression that random cars were stopping too, the way they do for a yard sale. No one who got out of them looked like Jenney.

"I'm not sure why. I just have to believe that whoever created that rule did it for a good reason."

"I can't believe you're not in my corner. When I'm finally happy." I felt like saying something harsh about Brenda Mason or one of Gordy's past girlfriends. Tight pants, overly concerned with status, cheated on the French exam. But I felt Gordy's hand on my back, calming me down.

"I am in your corner. I absolutely hope this works out, I would love to meet her someday, and I hope you guys get off to a good start. But I think you have a serious decision to make."

"What's that?" I didn't see how any decision regarding Jenney could be difficult.

"Can we sit out back?"

"Sure." We passed through the gate into the back-yard. Half a dozen plastic chairs were grouped around the statue of Athena. I turned two of them to face each other.

"You have to be honest in order to live with yourself," Gordy said. "You have to decide which is more important: this girl—Jenney, right?—or your volunteer work. Then you give up one and keep the other. So if she means more to you, you resign from Listeners, and that way you can keep your head up and be honest and aboveboard and not sneak around. Or ask your friends to sneak around."

I wanted to smile, but my face wouldn't make the right curve. I finished the dregs of my cocoa and reached for Gordy's NATIONAL GRID ENERGY DELIVERY mug. I shouldn't have said a word to Gordy about Jenney. I would go into the kitchen and wash the mugs and never speak to him again. No, I should have told him. He was right. Absolutely right. And just as I saw Listeners as a blip, a bump in the road, in the story of my happiness with Jenney, I saw quitting Listeners as a blip too. I could easily do that in order to be with the girl who made me happy.

"Do you know you're a pain sometimes?" I asked Gordon as we got up to join the others.

"Why?"

"Because you're right way too often."

"You wouldn't think that if you were wrong less often," Gordon said. "Hey, my dad and I will probably need to go in a few minutes. This show was great." He slapped my chest. "You come from a lot of talent, you know that?"

shrinkette

By one thirty Gordy was gone and there was no one I wanted to talk to. Mom, Marty, Linda, and Jodie were doing a great job chatting everyone up, so I took my bike out front and tinkered with it as people came and went. I dropped the bike and jogged to the road when I saw a tall, slim girl walk up in cowboy boots, corduroys, and a fleece vest, with a long braid hanging in front of one shoulder.

"Hi," I said.

"Hey." Was that her voice? I needed to hear more.

"How did you find out about this show?" I asked.

"I heard about it. . . . Word of mouth, I guess?"

"Jenney, it's me." I extended one hand. And then the other, for whatever she wanted to do with it.

"I'm sorry?" the girl said, touching my fingertips.

"It's me, Billy." I squeezed her gloved fingers and felt the smile nearly split my face open. "And I've got something big to tell you. I've decided to quit Listeners."

"Liza!" Dr. Fritz called. He was still here, having a

great time, apparently. He came out to the driveway and put his arm around the girl. "This is my daughter. Liza, this is Billy, the artist's son."

"Oh, I'm sorry," she said, shaking my hand. "I didn't know if I should say because my dad—"

"Because your dad has Billy's dad for a client," Dr. Fritz finished. "That's okay, Liza. Billy and I are old friends."

"What were you saying?" Liza asked me, taking off her gloves and smoothing her braid. "You had news about a decision? Or did you not mean for me to hear that? I'm sorry, this is so awkward."

"No, I'm sorry," I told her. They were Dad's people, not mine. I wished they would go into the garage where they belonged. "I confused you with someone else. You look a little like a friend of mine." I bent over my bike and pretended to adjust the brakes. "Enjoy the show, okay?"

together and apart

By four o'clock about eighty people had come and gone from the show. Dad had sold twelve paintings and gotten inquiries about lots more. Uncle Marty left, saying he had made a video of the whole day and couldn't wait to watch it with us. The sky was already dark.

"I hate for it to end," Jodie said. But Dad shut off the music and turned off the space heaters. Linda put the bios and price lists in a box, and I helped her carry in the card table.

With no guests to talk to, Mom sauntered to the back of the garage and positioned herself in front of *Diverted Horizon*. After twenty seconds, Dad noticed her there. He walked slowly to the wall and stood beside her. Jodie waved to Linda and me.

"Let's go inside," she said.

There would be time later to take down the poster and balloons. If Dad wanted me to, I would help him bring the artwork back inside. For now we left him and Mom to see what they needed to see.

PART 5

shift 10, december 6. call 45

Listeners. Can I help you?"

It's me.

"Jenney, where were you?"

I'm sorry. I couldn't make it.

"I waited and waited for you."

Oh, man.

"I kept looking up and down the street. I thought other people might be you. I wondered if you had gotten lost. Did you get lost?"

No, I didn't even leave the house Sunday. I couldn't get it together.

"Wow, I was really looking forward to it too. And you missed it. You missed an amazing day. You know what?"

What?

"It turns out my dad's a really good painter."

The show was good?

"Yeah! He even sold a bunch of things. People were

impressed. I feel like I can finally relax. But I wish you had been there. You might have been impressed too, and your opinion would have meant the most to me."

Oh, man.

"You're really quiet tonight."

I missed your dad's show.

"But that's not the most important thing. I have something really huge to tell you."

What is it?

"I'm quitting Listeners."

No! Don't do that!

"Why not?"

Below the office, in Hawthorne Square, a Salvation Army volunteer rang a bell. I had a bottle of iced tea and some peanut clusters from the snack cabinet. I felt at home. When I worked alone in my overtime hours, I felt like this place was my living room.

Because you're the best one.

"But I want to."

You do?

"I'm leaving Listeners for you."

Billy, don't do it. Don't leave Listeners.

"I'm glad to give it up. Do you know why?"

Why?

"Because I'm in love with you."

Oh . . . I'm surprised. But not surprised.

"What do you mean, 'not surprised'?"

I sort of thought so when you took the extra hours.

"I love you, Jenney. Do you love me?"

I can't take this in right now.

"Then don't. We'll put this conversation on hold and we'll talk when we see each other. It will be better then. So how was your weekend?"

It was bad. Really bad.

"Bad how? Is this why you didn't get to the show?"

I remembered the thing I had been trying to forget.

"What was that?"

About my brother, Tobey.

"I thought you were an only child."

I thought I was too.

"Who is Tobey?"

He's the brother I forgot. Melinda must have helped me remember him.

"But where is he now?"

He's gone. He was my little brother, and they killed him.

"Who did?"

My parents. My parents killed Tobey.

"When did this happen?"

Long ago, when I was five or six. This is the breakthrough. Melinda could tell I was breaking through. This is the thing I was supposed to remember.

The flashing of the lights on other lines was like a silent alarm. It seemed like all the fake-depressed people on the posters were listening. They were fake like Jenney's parents, and they had known all along.

I struck Margaret's doodle pad with my pen. Someone killed a child. Jenney had seen it. I had to protect Jenney.

"My God, Jenney, do the police know?"

They may or may not. They may have covered it up because of who my parents are.

"How did you figure this out?"

It was another sensory memory I kept having. Like the cold stone on my cheek and the cord around my neck. I remembered the name Tobey. And a baby's T-shirt. Oh my God.

"What's that noise? Are you laughing or crying?"

I'm not laughing.

"Oh, no. Jenney?"

What?

"You have to tell someone."

I'm telling you.

I can't be the only one who knows, I thought. A murder. This is too big for me. Without the college kids or Pep or Margaret or Richie, the room was too quiet. Where was everyone? I could use some advice right now. I felt like an astronaut tumbling in space with nothing to hold on to. Who could I call?

"You have to tell someone other than me. You have to tell Melinda. And you have to alert the authorities."

I don't know.

I wished I could reach into the phone and grab her. Grab her and put her in Margaret's chair so I could see her and make sure she was okay.

"We can research it together. I can help you. I can find the right people to call."

I doubt that that would work. You can't fight those two. Maybe it's time for me to stop fighting. Maybe now I have to admit that they won.

"How do you know they killed him?"

I kept hearing the name Tobey and seeing an infant-size St. Angus's T-shirt stained with blood. I was working on the memories with Melinda. Melinda kept asking me, "Who is Tobey? Who is Tobey?" And she said, "You don't have to protect them. You're grown up, and you're safe. You don't have to protect them anymore."

"I'm sorry. I'm so sorry. That's so terrible."

They killed him in the basement. I was unconscious while it happened. Then, when I woke up he was dead. It proves something about my parents. About their values and what's important to them.

"You have to tell the police about what you remember. Then it won't haunt you anymore. Then you can be free. You can walk away and start over. You can be like the college kids and go to St. Angus's. You can do anything you want."

I waited for Jenney to agree, to even consider agreeing.

"I think you can start over now, Jenney. You can turn your life around, just like you wanted to."

Nothing on the other end. I studied one of Margaret's doodles, a vase of flowers with big, circular petals.

"Jenney? I don't hear anything. Please say something to let me know you're there.

"Jenney, take a deep breath.

"Jenney, I'm worried about you. I want you to call every day from now on so I know you're all right. Call any time of day. Talk to whoever answers the phone. Margaret or Richie. Pep, especially Pep. Deke or Rosalys. Or the people on the other days. Okay?"

Okay.

"You're not feeling suicidal, are you?"

I might be.

She might be?

"Oh my God. What do you mean?"

Calm down. It isn't the end of the world.

"Yes, it is. You didn't mean to say yes, did you?"

I've given it my best shot. I tried and I failed. Now it's someone else's turn to try.

"Why didn't you tell me?"

I didn't want to upset you. You've been so worried already, about your dad's art show.

"I have no idea how you can say this."

It's just a feeling. You asked how I was feeling, remember?

At that moment the blood left my head. I was almost afraid to get up and go to my backpack.

"Wait a minute, Jenney," I said. "I have to get out my manual."

Okay.

She was waiting. For me to tell her what to do. I staggered to the coat rack for my pack. The room seemed too quiet. I could hear the rushing of traffic below the office, in Hawthorne Square. I went back to the table.

"Okay," I said. "This is stupid. No, I'm stupid. My hands are shaking."

It's not your fault, Billy.

"Just a minute. Now. Do you have any means of harming yourself?"

I have Valium. And some other stuff.

"You wouldn't really do that, would you? Jenney? Do you have the pills there? Do you have them in your hand?"

They're right here.

"How many do you have?"

I don't know. Do you want me to count them?

"Jenney ..."

I flipped through the sections of my booklet: "About Suicide." "Suicide Statistics." "Causes of Suicide." I had not looked at the booklet in a while and had trouble knowing which page or section would be best.

What?

"I'm panicking."

I'm sorry.

"Do you really want this to happen? Do you realize that if you die, your life ends?"

Vaguely. I don't feel like being clever right now.

"Suicide is only a ..."

I'm thinking of the people who are going to be sad tomorrow, and that's the only reason I'm still on the phone. There aren't that many. But you would be one of them.

I had found the section: "Questions to Ask a Caller Who Is Threatening to Commit Suicide."

"Don't even think about me. Where are you right now?"

At home.

"Exactly where?"

On the couch.

"In the living room?"

Yes.

"Where are the pills?"

In my hand.

"All right."

Good. I had the questions to ask. Jenney's answers matched my questions. We were following a sequence laid out in the book. I had been climbing a rock surface that offered me nothing, but I'd found a toehold again.

"Now the main thing I need you to do is to not be holding that bottle. I want you to put the phone down, move the pills to another room, like the bathroom, and then come back and talk to me again."

Okay. But I can only walk a little.

"Why's that?"

I already took some.

That was not a good answer. I didn't want to hear that. I felt the two of us pitching over the top of something. Like the Log Flume ride at Canobie Lake Park. The wooden dugout in a track filled with water labors slowly up the ride—*tickety, tickety, tick.* Then it reaches the top, and you're falling and inundated by water.

"When did you take them?"

Before I called.

I flipped back and forth in the manual, looking for "Caller Has Ingested." What was Valium? Was it an opiate? A narcotic? The book was too slow. I had to find something faster than the book.

"Oh my God. Where are Stacey and Rebecca tonight? Can you call them and ask them to take you to the emergency room?"

They don't want to hear from me anymore. They usually don't even answer when I call. Jenney and her problems.

"Would you give me their numbers, and the permission to call them? Will you let me call Stacey and Rebecca and ask them if they can help?"

They're sick of me. They don't want me to bug them. If

they wanted to see me, they would have come by here a long time ago.

"What about Melinda? She would help you if your life depended on it, right? Will she take you to the hospital?"

She's not allowed to see me. Look, don't do this. I don't want to think about my parents and the basement anymore. Tomorrow morning I'll be peaceful.

"What about neighbors? Is there anyone outside? Or down the hall? Anyone whose door you could knock on?"

I don't know them that well. I don't really have friends in this building.

"So what? Try to get to the doorway and talk to them anyway. I'll wait. They'll be completely smitten with you. They'll do whatever you ask them to."

I remember every compliment you ever gave me.

"You do?"

Especially when you said I was strong.

"You were strong, Jenney. You *are* strong. You're a fighter. Now get into the hall somehow, even if you have to drag yourself on your knees, and see if someone will take you to the emergency room. If you can't get into the hall, just go to the door, open it, and yell."

You need to stop this.

"I don't need to stop anything. You need to stop. You need to stop yourself from getting close to dying. You're the one who has to stop something. Jenney, why did you take those pills?"

I had my shot, and now it's over.

"What a stupid reason."

I began pacing, as far as the phone would allow. I picked

up the phone base and carried it as I walked. I wasn't used to a phone with a cord. I looked out the window as if I could see Jenney. If only I were at her apartment, or somewhere near her, I could do something real. Something to help.

I'm through with fighting. I just want the pain to end.

"That's ridiculous. I'm sorry, that sounded judgmental. Jenney, are you still there?"

I'm going to lie down.

"Don't lie down, Jenney. Don't go to sleep. Just keep walking. Walk around the apartment while I talk to you. I want you to call 911. The police will come and take you to the emergency room. Will you do that?"

I'm really tired.

"I want you to hang up, call 911, and call me back."

Don't bother, Billy.

"If you won't call 911, will you let me call 911? Will you give me your address and let me do that?"

It doesn't seem worth the trouble.

"It is worth the trouble. You only think it isn't because you took those pills. I'm going to call 911 right now. May I have your permission to do that? Are you still there?"

Jenney didn't give me the address. In fact, she stopped responding.

I placed lines 1 and 3 on hold. The office was quiet except for cars slowing in the square. At this hour, not even the elevator ran. I swept the snacks off the table and onto the floor. I lay my head down on my workstation.

I imagined how different things might be if it were two hours ago, if Jenney had announced her intention while Margaret and Richie were on duty. Would they have coached me differently, and would my response to Jenney have been different? If Margaret had been here, would the police have Jenney now?

I left line 1, which I never had the right to man anyway. Margaret was line 1. I was a pretender and a usurper. I sat for a second at my old spot at line 3, with all three lines on hold, and wondered what to do. I had been happy as the number three guy. Why did I insist on being more?

outside

Outside, I was closer to where Jenney was. Or at least not staying where she was not.

I started by primitively peering around my cave. Two blocks to the left. Three blocks to the right. No surprise, she wasn't there. My bike was locked to a parking meter. Nearby was a lighted bus shelter with a schedule and map, but no routes running at this hour of night. And so many streets in our town that I've never heard of. But some large being—call It God, call It the best part of me—was holding me in Its hands.

flying

Sometimes you move so fast, there's only exertion. You don't know what you're doing other than moving forward. You only know that something inside you is compelled, is alive, is breathing, is productive, and motion is its only product. Now I was the one moving. People froze in crosswalks as I flew by. Cars rolled when the light changed, then saw me and thought better of it. Because sometimes the world reshaped itself to one person's will, and will is always moving.

compass

I pedaled into the honking, blaring center of Hawthorne. Across the Common, through its cheesy wooden processional arch. I felt totally off-manual. No notes, no tips, no scraps of paper, just my bare hands on the handlebars. Above me, a half moon, like God's partly covered flashlight.

What did I know about Jenney that could help me find her? I knew so little, and because I was panicking, the facts flew out of my head each time I tried to get hold of them. Mother is a socialite, father writes books. No, mother writes books, father has a TV station. Well known, well connected, lots of parties. But I didn't know their last name. Friends Stacey and Rebecca, didn't know their last names. Therapist Melinda, didn't know her last name but could possibly find it on a list of therapists somewhere, if she was listed as a therapist with first name Melinda instead of M and didn't live too far away.

Just beyond the Common was the fire department. Four fire trucks, one van. Someone stood in the open door of one of the trucks. I waited for him to finish what he was doing, but then I saw it was not a person but a pair of empty boots and rolled-down pants waiting for someone to jump into them. I schooned to the office marked VISITORS and found a firefighter behind the desk watching *Boardwalk Empire.* Another one was eating the last slice from a box of pizza.

"This is kind of a weird question," I said, "but do you know of any caterers in town that do clambakes?"

"Woodbine's?" the one behind the desk suggested.

"I don't think it's them. I don't think it's a restaurant, I think it's people who bring the clams to your company or picnic or whatever."

"Beauport Clam Company?"

"Is it—is it run by a woman who used to own a breakfast place with 'Egg' in the name?"

"The Incredible Egg," the pizza one said.

"What is the woman's name?"

"Marion Sibley." These guys were pretty quick. They waited for more questions, as if tonight were trivia night.

"May I use your telephone book?"

"Do you have a sudden craving for clams?" the one at the desk asked. He laughed. Then I made a face, and he gave me the phone book from inside his desk.

I couldn't waste even a second joking with these guys. Precious seconds were slipping by. In fact, maybe I should have asked the firefighters for help. They were *real* lifesavers, after all. But what about confidentiality? I decided that if five minutes went by and I made no progress, I would tell them I was from Listeners and what I was doing. But as long as I had a chance of finding Jenney in time, I wanted to save her myself.

I called Marion Sibley's house. Thank God, a woman answered.

"I'm sorry to bother you late at night," I said. "You have a new person working for you named Jenney, right?" She paused, and I realized that even Jenney's first name, like Kevin's, could be fake. If that were the case, I'd have nothing to go on, no clues even for the firefighters.

"Why?" the woman asked.

"My name is Billy Morrison, and I have something I have to drop off for her, but she forgot to give me her address. Please don't think this is too strange. I'm not a weirdo or anything; I'm a new friend of Jenney's and I have something of hers that she needs back and I don't have her address or phone number, and this is something she needs right away, desperately." I didn't tell the woman that the thing I would drop off for Jenney was the rest of her life.

"I guess I can give you her cell number," the woman said, "and she can decide whether to see you or not."

"No, please, just the address. If you have it on her job application or somewhere. Please, I'm begging you. Jenney needs me to do this."

The woman left for a minute. Then she came back and said, "She lives at Maple Ledge. I hope it was okay for me to tell you. . . ." But I was yelling "Thank you!" and closing my phone.

Now I had another problem. I'd heard of Maple Ledge but never seen it. "Can you tell me where Maple Ledge is?" I asked the firefighters. "I'm in kind of a hurry."

"We specialize in hurries. It's right across the street."

"It is?"

"Sure." The firefighter walked me back to the sidewalk. "See the sign saying 'Hawthorne Housing Authority'? That's Maple Ledge."

"That's it?"

"That's it."

Three more firefighters came downstairs, having finished their supper, I guess, and bored, to see what I wanted.

"That your bike outside?" one asked. "I hope you're wearing a helmet."

I strapped on my headgear while observing the place where Jenney lived. Maple Ledge was for people without much money. My first-grade teacher lived there. And Linda's friend Marcia Jane Bailey. In all our conversations, I never pictured Jenney living downtown, just two blocks from my office. Maybe because her parents were rich. But Jenney didn't want anything from them. Her loyalty wasn't for sale.

In minutes I would be at Jenney's door. How long would it take for her to open it? Then how soon for her to know it was me? Would she need medical attention? Would she have to be revived? As I waited by her bedside for her eyes to open, would she be puzzled at the sight of me, then recognize my voice the minute I spoke? Would she say, "I can't believe you saved me," and then we'd be like on the phone, only better?

Breathe, Jenney, breathe.

the ledge

Plastic toys, tricycles, and radios. A few people here and there, meeting, leaving, smoking on their front steps in the cold. The residents emitted a prickle of inhospitality. I decided to ask the first person I saw if they knew Jenney, but the first three were men, and two squinted at me, and I felt protective of her, not knowing if they were nice people. Maybe they were simply wary of outsiders, but Maple Ledge reminded me of war photos where everyone is hardened, and you wonder, Where did the friendly people go? Did some kind of high-tech bomb destroy anyone you might want to borrow a dollar from? I wished I could find my old teacher or Marcia Jane Bailey.

At the third building I saw two girls on the steps. I glided in close, using Triumph as a scooter. Both girls had three earrings in each ear and almost no eyebrows, like a dotted line saying "Place eyebrows here." *Was* one of them Jenney? Did she wake up and come outside to revive herself? I hovered, listening for her voice. But these girls were both smoking, so they couldn't be Jenney. She was a swimmer, after all.

"Excuse me," I said. "I'm looking for somebody."

"That usually means trouble."

"Well, it could in this case, but I hope not." I had to hurry but sensed they needed softening up. "How are you ladies tonight?"

"Can't complain."

A picket gate separated us. "May I?"

Swinging the gate open, I felt all of Maple Ledge's eyes on me.

"Do you know a girl named Jenney who lives here? A bit older than me?"

"A big girl with honey-colored hair?"

"I don't know," I said. Then I regretted how odd that sounded. I had to protect my connection with Jenney. Sure, I could blast through Maple Ledge with an alarm blaring, yelling, "Likely! Likely!" But tomorrow morning when she woke up, Jenney would have lost her privacy.

"I'm a friend of hers, and I knew she was going to be home tonight, and I wanted to surprise her."

"But you don't know what she looks like?"

"No."

"Are you her boyfriend?"

"No."

"You met online, then."

"I'd rather not say. But I think she would want to see me if she knew I was here."

"Why don't you call her and find out where she is?"

"I don't have her number."

"She's your girlfriend, but you don't know her number."

"Maybe she doesn't want to be found," said the girl on the right.

I realized that although the girls appeared to be sisters, they were actually a mother and daughter who looked the same age. The kind that were best friends. Real parent-child friendships were rare. They were usually just wishful thinking. On the part of the parent, not the kid.

I wished I had Gordy with me. It would have been comforting to hear my name among strangers. And Gordy would have known how to talk to these women. Unlike me, he had a knack for putting people at ease. What would Gordy say?

"You know, ladies, when I first rode up here, I thought you were sisters or friends. I had no idea you were mother and daughter."

"Everyone says that," the mother replied, unimpressed. "You met online, didn't you? That's why you don't know her number. I don't see why anyone would meet online. There are a lot of wackos out there."

"I'm not a wacko."

"Maybe not," says the younger one. "But you're not anyone's dream date, either. If you're taking Jenney out, is she going to ride on your handlebars?"

I unstrapped my helmet. My head was sweating. I needed to plan the next move. If only this scenario was happening on the phone instead of in person. At Listeners I was great at opening people up. I was a master.

I should have stuck with Ye Olde Girlfriend-Boyfriend Template. I could have talked my way past the neighbors and I would be in the apartment by now. Breathe, Jenney.

"What if I am her boyfriend?"

"Then she's a lucky girl," the younger woman said.

The mother exhaled a warning plume. "We've talked to Jenney a few times. She never mentioned a boyfriend."

"I can imagine how you must be feeling. Suspicious. Worried. Maybe impatient." I rolled back and forth, listing their prejudices like a cagey courtroom lawyer, except on wheels. "But look. I'm just here because I'm worried about Jenney. Look in my eyes. Can't you tell I'm not one of the bad guys?"

"It's a good thing you came by, actually," the mother said. "What is your name?"

"Benjy."

"I don't think Jenney has a lot of friends. We spoke to her a few hours ago, and she seemed pretty fried. She said it was a bad day and she was going back to bed."

I felt dread sweep from my feet to my head as if my body were filling with sand. She should have told me sooner. I was the person she should have told. I was starting to hate myself.

"Rest your bike against the fence there," the mother said. "I'll tell you what you say when you get upstairs."

"I should get up there right away."

"Listen to me for a minute. She's independent. She might pretend everything's fine."

"Right. What's the apartment number?"

"Thirty."

"What building is that in?"

She jerked her thumb toward the building beside us and let me in the front door with her key.

Jenney, I'm here.

thirty

The hallway smelled like cigarette smoke and litter boxes. The heat seemed too high, and someone had left a window open in the staircase. I heard the furnace clanging underneath us. Beside the door marked thirty, polka-dotted snowboots and an umbrella rested on a plastic tray.

I knocked on the door. "Jenney, it's Billy. I know you told me not to come, but I did anyway, because I was worried. Jenney?" I looked for a doorbell or buzzer but couldn't find one. I must have passed it in the lobby.

"Jenney, it's Billy. Don't you recognize my voice? It's me. For real. Can you believe it? I'm here. Now let me in. Let me in and we'll talk." I tried not to shout or sound like I was arguing. I didn't want a crowd to gather.

"Okay, we can talk through the door if you want. You don't have to let me in. It would be nice to meet in person someday, but I don't really care. It's up to you. Bring a chair to the door and sit down if you're tired. We'll talk right through the door.

"Hey, I have a cell phone with me. Why don't I give you the number?

"Hear this? I have my cell phone. It's 978-555-0136. You sit there, I'll sit out here, and we'll talk. Here I go. Getting comfortable. Waiting for your call. Operators are standing by.

"Did I give you that number too fast? Just pick up the phone, Jenney, if you hear me. You don't have to write anything down. I'll say the numbers one at a time, and you punch them in. 9. 7. 8. 5. 5. 5. 0. 1. 3. 6. . . . 9. 7. 8. 5. 5. 5. 0. 1. 3. 6. . . . 9. 7. 8. 5. 5. 5. 0. 1. 3. 6.

"You don't have to be afraid of me, Jenney. I won't even come in. We don't need to see each other. Just say something. Tell me what you're doing right now.

"Do you want me to go away, Jenney? If you're all right and you want me to go away and leave you alone, knock twice.

"Knock twice, Jenney.

"If you can't get to the door, knock twice on the wall wherever you are. Knock twice.

"Knock once.

"Are you tired? Just knock once.

"Knock like this. Hear this?"

The apartment was too quiet. If only I heard a sound. One sound. Groaning. Furniture moving. Anything.

I didn't think I was going to save her.

"Jenney, give me something. Give me something I can work with."

I opened my phone and called 911.

the door opens

I waited for the police, looking out a curtainless window in a staircase that smelled like disinfectant and old trash. I heard the siren, and a scowling nub of people in the playground dispersed. The first cop came up the stairs, a tall police-woman with a blond crew cut and long earrings, named, according to her badge, Lieutenant Tall. Behind her was Officer Novello, who I recognized as a friend of Marty's. He came to our house in the winter when I abandoned Dad to attend a blues concert. He must have thought I was a pain in the butt, first disappearing from where I needed to be, then showing up where I had no business being.

"You the friend?" the woman said.

I answered yes.

"Lieutenant Tall of the Hawthorne Police Department. Step aside, please."

"Police! Anybody here?" She tried the knob. She pressed her ear against the door. Then she knocked. "Police! Anybody here?"

She turned to me again. "Have you spoken to your friend since you talked to our dispatcher?"

"No."

"The fire squad is coming to get this door open."

Almost immediately two firefighters were upstairs too, including the one who'd sat at the desk and given me directions. He didn't seem surprised to see me. Maybe nothing surprised them. He inserted a claw in the doorjamb and struck it with a flatheaded ax. The door opened.

Behind the scratched-up door I glimpsed a normal living room with a nautical-style clock, a television, a laptop computer beside an empty KFC bucket. A couch, some blankets.

"Miss? Miss?" Lieutenant Tall called. "Jenney? Are you here?"

Then they moved through the apartment, pushing doors open. A closet. A bathroom. A bedroom.

"There's someone in here," a firefighter said.

"Stay out there," Officer Novello told me. "Don't come in."

"There's someone in the bed," Lieutenant Tall said. "Miss? Are you Jenney?"

Novello came out to the hall. "Don't go in."

He talked on his radio? To police headquarters? To an ambulance that would now turn back? But Jenney's voice was nowhere to be heard, and I dialed Pep's cell number and left a message of two words: "Jenney's dead." Officer Novello wrapped his arm around my shoulder and led me to the stairs. Otherwise I would have stood there, listening, forever.

news

Why didn't I let Jenney talk?

Why didn't I let her tell me she had taken the pills?

I stayed in my room all day Wednesday, asking myself those questions, hoping no one would find me or call. I pretended to be sick. Mom, Dad, Linda, and Jodie hardly noticed my hiding. They were still high from Sunday, and they probably thought I was just avoiding the show again. On Monday, Dad had decided to leave most of the artwork up for another week. He was going to photograph and catalogue the art and invite some Boston gallery owners out for a visit.

Why didn't you let Jenney talk, you imbecile?

Why didn't you listen to her? You ass.

I walked in circles from room to room. This was the way my father had paced last winter, talking only to the demons inside himself.

That evening, Mom was reading the *Hawthorne-Beacon Times*, criticizing the grammar on the op-ed page.

Linda was cutting pictures from a magazine to decoupage a lunchbox. Mom held the paper up, and I saw the back of it.

"What's wrong?" Linda asked. "Billy, you look really weird."

She looked from me to the paper.

So that was Jenney's face.

hawthorne woman found dead

Jennefer Alves, nineteen. Daughter of Jordan and Takano Alves. Hawthorne High graduate, champion swimmer, employed by Beauport Clam Company. Yes, that was my Jenney. The article didn't mention suicide. It referred to her death as "sudden" and "unexpected." It identified her parents as the owners of a wholesale lobster business but said nothing about the books, the fancy parties, or the TV station. The article didn't mention a brother named Tobey. Or her friends: Stacey. Rebecca. Me.

98.

how did you help this incoming?

By answering the phone when it was her.

By always being happy to hear her voice.

By not knowing her before, so she could explain herself to me from the very beginning.

By liking or praising whatever I saw in her to like or praise.

By some of those things being things no one else might have thought of.

what could you have done better?

I know what you mean by "done better." But you have to look at the basic qualities that each person brings to the job. And you have to assume that those qualities will come into play. In other words, that a volunteer is not a senseless automaton pushing buttons and burping platitudes. If that's what you want, why don't you fire everybody and set up an automated answering system like you get at a bank or some other place that's not trying to help people? At least they're not pretending.

Okay, I know I seem a little angry now. Give me a few minutes.

100.

what questions do you have before you hear our decision?

I guess I have trouble understanding how easily you can put a limit on the amount of yourself you're willing to give to someone. In fact, many people believe that the most admirable form of human behavior is a heroic sacrifice, in which you push yourself to extremes in order to cheat death of its claim on another person's life, throwing yourself repeatedly to the brink of exhaustion and being washed back limp. I suppose you, Pep, believe hoarding your compassion allows you to save some for tomorrow and the day after that. But I guess I've always thought compassion is one of those self-perpetuating resources—the more you use, the more you have.

listener of the year: not

I'd like to say that my efforts with Jenney, which could not have been more sincere, led me to an award of some sort. But life isn't often like that. I should have realized that Pep wasn't made of normal teenage stuff. I had expected her to wail, shed tears, leap in her car, and drive across town to hug me, buy a cross or a teddy bear or a bouquet for the door to Jenney's building, and act the way people generally act after a death. Instead, she said, "I know it's difficult, but there was nothing more you could do."

Then the executive board called a meeting that they called a "process exploration" but which I thought of as a "court-martial." Pep tried to pull the story out of me by emphasizing my feelings: "What were you feeling when that happened?" "What were you feeling when you decided that?" But the other board members, three college students and two professionals in their thirties, listened with an expression that said, "What were you thinking?"

"Are you aware," said Gerald, a professor of social

work at Hawthorne State, "that when news of this gets out, some Incomings will feel that they can never trust us with confidential information again?"

"I guess so."

"We're already getting calls," Pep added. "Some Daily Incomings have called to ask which Listener was prowling around Maple Ledge the night a girl died."

"They'll figure it out," a college student said. "They have an uncanny sense for discerning what goes on around here. They have this quivering, like, antenna that senses the slightest possible change. They'll figure out it was you."

"How will they figure it out?"

"When you're no longer on the schedule," Pep said.

I knew that was coming, but I hadn't gotten around to thinking about it yet.

"We don't have a choice," Pep said.

"Remember," Gerald said, "what happens at Listeners—"

Stays at Listeners. Along with my badge, my key, and my procedures manual. The rest of the meeting was an avalanche of nots. I stopped fighting.

102.

blackout

I stood on the Common with my bike and waited for them to end the tribunal, gather their papers, and turn out the lights. When that last yellow square was extinguished, the top floor of Cabot Hall blended into the surrounding darkness as if it had never existed. As if I'd never been there at all.

103.

in the cemetery (my painting)

Black and black, with two bright dots that could be Stacey and Rebecca.

coda

Officially, I didn't know her.

So I didn't attend the funeral. But I did wait two blocks from the funeral home for the procession to go by. Ten cars, five limo and five civilian, with magnetic flags on the hoods saying FUNERAL. I allowed several nonfuneral cars that had waited respectfully at the intersections to join the flow of traffic. Then I made a distant, unofficial end to Jenney's parade. When the limos stopped in the cemetery, I rode past. I pretended to be someone who was riding through recreationally, which is forbidden in the cemetery but which I've done before. One or two mourners glared at me, and I looked away, pretending ignorance. But I saw two girls who hid their bright dresses under black coats and their bright hair under hats and sunglasses, and who howled and hung on to each other like they were going to collapse. So maybe they did care about her more than she thought, or maybe they were calling attention to themselves, or maybe their central nervous systems were stimulated by the drama. Spiraling away from where the mourners would leave Jenney, I had an aerial view of myself as a peripheral detail, a small, mechanical figure. Someone who rides in circles while others are living their lives.

deadline

The day after the funeral I said nothing to my parents and Linda. I felt dry and hollow, like a gourd. I had seeds instead of guts, and if someone had shaken me, I would have rattled. But I went to school as usual.

In music history class I sat beside Gordon. Dani Solomon, a tennis player with red hair, got up to do her presentation on Klezmer music. She wore a white skirt with fringe that swung as she walked.

"Ooh," Gordy whispered as she passed, "there she is."

Dani talked about how this type of music began at Jewish weddings and borrowed tunes from Roma (Gypsy) bands. How the instruments were meant to sound like human voices laughing and crying. How Klezmer clarinet had influenced the first note in Gershwin's *Rhapsody in Blue*. After hitting the play button for each music sample on her CD player, Dani twisted her hands and waited for the music to end.

Mr. Gabler walked toward my desk. Naturally, I hadn't

done anything about my paper since Dad's show. How could I? I tried to figure out what to tell him. I wouldn't say that someone I loved had died. I would say that although Mr. Gabler thought school was my big life or a stepping stone to it, my big life was actually elsewhere.

Just as Gabler arrived at my desk there was a knock at the door. A police officer came into the classroom and spoke to Gabler, then asked me to come with him and removed me from the class.

the story of emma p. braumann

We rode in Officer Novello's cruiser, with no siren, to a coffee shop opposite the state fish pier.

"Let's grab some breakfast," Novello said.

When the waitress came, Novello held the menu in front of his face without reading it. I saw him watch a park next to the pier where drug deals were reputed to go down.

After two cars left the park he lowered his menu and eyed me with his head tilted, the way people express thoughts like, You're putting me on or Now tell me something I don't know.

"Unbelievable," he said.

"What is?"

"You're exactly like your portrait."

I shrugged. "My portrait is exactly like me."

"You know, every person who comes into that bar, Marty walks them around your portrait in a hundred-and-eighty-degree arc. 'Do you see it yet?' he says. 'Do you see it?'"

"He sure seems to get a kick out of it," I said. I was glad Dad had decided to give Marty the painting for free.

"Do you know the story of Emma P. Braumann?" he asked me once we'd ordered our food.

"No idea." I hadn't really thought of the person behind the snack cabinet.

"I'll tell you. Emma P. Braumann was a very nice lady, about my mother's age. She would have been. If she had lived. But she didn't live. Which was the whole thing. She was a jumper. Right off the bridge there, before the chain-link fence went up.

"Not many people know the whole story. The story is that Emma P. Braumann's dear friend Mary Alice was engaged to someone in the service. They had been childhood sweethearts. In fact, the boy lived right across the street. Hale Street. He was only a month or so from the end of his tour of duty. And then he would return home and they would be married. So Mary Alice is at home, idly looking out the window. She sees an official car pull up across the street. A soldier in uniform gets out and for a minute she's excited, thinking it's him. But then she sees it's a dress uniform. Not the fatigues he would wear for a visit home. So who is it?

"The soldier goes up the walk. Removes his hat and rings the bell. The fiancé's mother answers the door. And then of course Mary Alice realizes. The army has sent someone to tell the family that the fiancé is dead. They wouldn't come to Mary Alice's, house of course. They would go to the mother's because the mother is the next of kin. Mary Alice runs across the street to her fiancé's family, wild with grief. She spends the afternoon attempting to comfort the mother, and then Emma comes over and sits with the two of them and suddenly Mary Alice says she doesn't want to live anymore and she's going to throw herself off the bridge. She gets in the car, parks on the near side of the bridge. Emma had insisted on following her on foot and saw her climb the railing. Mary Alice jumped, and the river started carrying her along. The sun was just setting and she was being pulled along, waving her arms, still quite visible because of her pale yellow blouse. Emma, without even thinking, jumped in right after her. She was a strong swimmer, after all; she came from a line of fishermen. It was a long drop, but in she went. But she hit the water at the wrong angle and was instantly killed."

"What a shame." That explained Emma's Listeners connection. I piled pieces of egg yolk onto an English muffin.

"She was a true hero. But you're right, what a shame."

"So she tried to rescue her friend. And that's why her family is so proud? Her nieces and nephews?"

"Very proud. And rightly so."

"But I have a question." Preparing to talk, I sipped some juice and wiped my mouth.

"What's that?" He opened his hands toward me as if I were a witness in the box.

"You mentioned the sight of Mary Alice riding the current in a pale yellow blouse. That was Emma's viewpoint. If Emma drowned, how does anyone know that's what she saw? How do we know that the pale yellow was still visible? How do we know she was waving? How did all that get into the police notes?"

I resumed eating. So much for this urban, or suburban, legend.

"It didn't."

"How do we know, then?"

"Because that's how Mary Alice told it."

"Mary Alice lived?" I popped my head back in surprise, just the response he was looking for.

"Yes, she did live. She thought better of it and allowed herself to be carried toward shore, behind a house with a private dock downstream near the railroad bridge. She pulled herself onto the pilings and lay there until help arrived. She was taken to the hospital for emotional exhaustion but was physically fine. In fact, after a few hours in the hospital and a change into dry clothes, she walked home and went directly across the street to help the woman who was supposed to become her mother-in-law. People were tough in those days. And they walked a lot more."

"That's unbelievable."

"And after an appropriate interval of paying respect to the fallen, she met someone else and married and had children. And she's my mother." He slapped the table.

"Mary Alice is your mother?"

"That's right. You know the Mary Alice of Mary Alice's Variety?"

"Next to the hospital?" I pointed with my thumb.

"That's my mother."

Novello finished his coffee and handed me a slice of

bacon without using utensils. "There's a lot to learn in a small town. You can never get to the end of it."

I nibbled the bacon. The waitress refilled his coffee and left the check.

"There's one other version of the story," Officer Novello continued.

"What's that?" I wondered if he always told stories or if he knew I would be receptive because I had been a Listener.

"There's a version that says that Emma wasn't trying to rescue Mary Alice. That Emma was in love with the same guy. Mary Alice's boyfriend. It was my mother's fiancé who got killed, but Emma loved him too. So even though she had no prospects along that line, when she heard about the death, she took her own life. Because, you know, there had been some kind of long-term fantasy there. Which now was not going to be realized."

"She wasn't a hero?" How complicated people's motivations could be.

"Everybody's a hero. Is what I'm learning."

"Is everybody a villain, too?"

"Too neat."

I still had one egg left, so I ordered another English muffin and more jelly. Someone in a jacket and tie walked by the window and looked at the cop, then at me. Officer Novello waved to him: Move along.

"You know," he said, putting away his wallet, "I've gone to calls like your friend's half a dozen times, and I still have the same reaction. I can't fathom what could be so bad that someone would want to leave this earth."

"I guess not." I almost could, though. I heard what Jenney's voice was like when she lost Melinda. Maybe those of us who couldn't fathom it were the lucky ones.

"Should we tell your mom and dad what happened?" he asked, leaning toward me as if he were my new friend. I mimed lip-zipping, then folded my arms on the table. "I'm not telling anybody anything. Besides, my parents are riding high right now. I wouldn't want to ruin everything by giving them bad news."

We got up. Officer Novello patted his thighs, checking for all the paraphernalia he had to carry. There must be stuff there that people have no idea of. High-tech, secret, spy-type stuff. Like me, and maybe like others in our town, he was a carrier of secrets.

"All right, well, if you don't want to talk to your parents, just talk to somebody. Okay?"

macaroni yet again

Andy and I tucked into our plates of American chop suey. Mitchell had a meatball sub and two containers of milk. Gordy had brought corned beef with sauerkraut and Russian dressing.

"How's it going at Life Savers, R?" Mitchell asked in between milks.

"We parted ways," I said casually. "You know, philosophical differences."

"I'm sorry about your friend," Andy said, looking earnest, like I was an adult he had to impress.

"What friend?" My spine stiffened. Had they heard about Jenney?

"Margaret," he explained. "The Listener. I'm sorry about what I did to Margaret." The apology was a long time in coming. I wondered if Gordy or Mitchell had put him up to it.

"I can't talk to you about her," I said.

Andy stopped eating and pressed his head against the

back of his wrist. His fork, in this awkward position, pro-truded from his forehead like a cockatiel crest.

"But did you ever stop to think that maybe I called because I needed to call?"

"What do you mean?"

"Think about it. Why does someone call a suicide hot-line, even as a prank? Doesn't it have to be a cry for help, even if they're covering up?"

He had a point, actually. I had assumed that his call was just to make fun of us, but I shouldn't have assumed anything at all. To be truly compassionate I would have to try living on the Andy-as-Hagrid Planet. I put down my fork. "Are you all right?" I asked.

He whispered, *"No."*

"Andy? Were you having a bad day the day you called? It's all right, Andy. You can talk to me."

Andy's face started to redden, and his mouth crumpled into a crooked line.

"I always seem to push people away," he said. "Even you guys. Even the people I really like."

"You think you push people away sometimes." I reached across the table and rested one hand on his shoulder.

Andy stabbed my arm with his fork. "Gotcha!"

Mitchell and Gordy laughed, or maybe just made sounds of astonishment.

"I wasn't in the mood for that," I told them.

"Tasteless, yes," Mitchell said. "But you have to admit, funny."

"I'm an idiot," I said. "I should have known you guys

were pulling my chain. Andy would never be serious about calling a help line."

"Sure I would," Andy said. He stopped eating and folded his arms in front of his tray.

"Oh, yeah? What would you call about?"

Andy looked right into my eyes. "That of all your friends you like me the least. And you remind me of that every single day."

The edges of the caf seemed to dissolve until nothing existed but Andy and me staring at each other. I wished I could stab him with a fork to break the mood.

"What would you call about, Mitchell?" Andy asked.

"He wouldn't," I said. The tomato sauce tasted sweet against the soggy, chewy elbows of pasta.

Mitchell sat back and ran one thumb under his suspenders. "I'm not suicidal over it," he said, "but my dad just moved out."

"No way." Mitchell's parents and my parents had been in and out of each other's houses for my whole childhood. "Wow, Mitchell, that's huge. I'm really sorry. Why didn't you tell me?"

"You seemed preoccupied," he said.

"I'm not anymore," I told him.

The four of us sat there, tearing bread, gulping soda, and watching the parade of girls and guys and their sometimes knowable, sometimes mysterious lives.

bearings

I signed a piece of paper.

But maybe I could tell one person, someone I knew would keep it a secret.

"So you know I'm not at Listeners anymore," I began on the way home from school. Gordon was walking while I rode really slowly on my bike. I didn't know how much I would say. I hated burdening other people with my problems.

"Because of the girl?" he asked.

"Yeah. But it's not what you think."

"What's going on? Are you two together?"

"No, we're not together. She's gone."

"Gone where?"

"She's dead. She died."

Gordy glanced at me, then looked out at the water and nodded. I felt Jenney separating from me and joining the ranks of all the other people who had died. She had more in common with Gordy's mom now than she had with me.

The wind along the boulevard made goose bumps on the surface of the gray water, then whistled past our ears. I smelled damp pavement and beer from the yuppie micro-brewery nearby. I stopped my bike at the wall that listed the names of Hawthorne's fishermen who had died at sea, and Gordon and I climbed up and sat on the wall.

"The girl you liked died," he said, "and you weren't going to tell me?"

"I signed a confidentiality agreement. Like you said, I had to play by the rules. I wasn't allowed to discuss her. I wanted to do things right. I shouldn't even have told you her name."

Gordy hopped down from the wall and stood close enough to me that he blocked my entire view.

"I know she died, Billy," he said. "It was in the news-paper. A girl named Jennefer, a few years older than us, who was a swimmer. I've been waiting for you to say something."

"I'm sorry. I . . ." Maybe I told myself I had a knack for dealing with people, but in fact I was totally inadequate. Maybe I had what Andy described: I was always pushing away the people I liked.

Gordy turned his back and looked out at the har-bor, which already was almost dark. The lighthouse at the end of the stone breakwater that enclosed the harbor had begun its sweep, sending a ray of light around in a circle, over and over, the visual equivalent of the tolling of a bell.

"No," said Gordon. "I'm the one who's sorry. I have no right to be mad. I know she was really important to you.

I just don't understand the way you think sometimes."

I banged my heels against the monument. The darkness gave us privacy and connected me to the nights with Jenney. It made me want to talk.

"I don't know if I was thinking or not. But I'm starting to realize that I feel really bad now. I mean . . . I almost feel bad enough to call Listeners myself."

The captain of a fishing boat told me once that seasickness climbs up your back, and you can stop it at different points along the way. But once it reaches the back of your neck you're a goner. I realized now that the same was true of crying.

Gordy stood beside me at the wall. "Why don't you tell me what happened?" he asked when I was done. "I mean, as much as you think you should say?"

I started telling him everything, about doing a great job for several weeks and being one of the best people there, listening to Jenney, getting to know her. How I started to care for her a huge amount and said some things I shouldn't have said. Then about Jenney getting more desperate, the pills, looking for Jenney, and the police finding her.

"It sounds like you blame yourself for what happened," Gordy said, checking my face.

"I do," I answered.

A foghorn sounded from the lighthouse. I had to admit that it was one of my favorite sounds.

"I'm trying to figure out who *is* responsible," Gordy said, "but it's pretty complicated. What do you think?"

"Her parents."

"They don't sound like the greatest. If what she said is true."

"Her therapist, Melinda. I wonder if she feels the same way I do today. Like, if she can't stop puzzling over everything she did and deciding what she should have done differently."

"Maybe she played a part. But the full responsibility?"

"Her two friends?" I thought of Stacey and Rebecca falling apart at the funeral. How long had it been since they were real friends to Jenney?

"It doesn't sound like it."

"I think I have it," I said.

"What do you have?"

"Jenney herself is responsible."

"That's what I think too. She made the final decision. Whether it was a good one or a bad one is on her shoulders. I think she made a bad call."

"Because it was a permanent solution to a temporary problem."

We both listened to the foghorn a while more, and I started rolling my bike again.

Gordon and I stopped at his house for nachos and soda. I noticed Dad's *Three Dories* hanging above the bookcase in the living room.

I rode home the long way, from Beauport back to Hawthorne past Murray into Intervale and back again. I wondered whether Jenney's problems really had been temporary. The newspaper article made it sound like her parents may not have been as rich and important as she had made them out to be. If not, maybe what she said, or believed, about Tobey also was not true. Maybe that memory of Tobey would have tortured her for the rest of her life. Or maybe she would have let go of it, and some other problems would have come into her life. Maybe peace was never in the cards for Jenney.

I could have checked her stories by doing some research. But so what if Jenney hadn't been telling the truth? Like the length of her legs, the color of her hair, and the size of her eyes in relation to her mouth, those facts didn't really matter. They made no difference in how well I knew Jenney.

improvements

I ran into Pep in, of all non-life-and-death places, Schneider Lumber, our town hardware store. She was with her roommate, shopping for plant hangers. I was doing errands with Mom, and I felt neutered by the parental presence even more than I did by Pep's. Pep and I stared in different directions—we weren't supposed to know each other, since our acquaintance stemmed from a secret organization—then met by intentional accident in front of the Venetian blinds.

"Hey," she said.

"Hey."

She adjusted one blind, opening and closing, letting light in, shutting it out.

"How are things at command central?" I asked.

"The same. Naturally I can't reveal anything about any specific Incoming or Incomings."

"Naturally. The same staffers there?"

"Pretty much the same."

I flipped through a booklet of color samples. "Any promising new people?"

"Two recruits still in training. One looks like a hot-shot. But you never know."

"No one ever knows much. For sure. This is the most general conversation I've ever had in my life." Heat rose to the back of my neck. I still didn't entirely agree that I should have been let go.

Pep shrugged and glanced in the direction of her roommate.

"So, how will you spend your extra time now?" Pep asked, using her best Salton manners.

"Actually, I'm here to pick up some things for Habitat for Humanity." I pulled a random paper from my pocket and brandished it.

"Is that woman with Habitat too?" she asked, angling her head toward Mom because she was too polite to point.

"That woman's my mom. She's the director of a museum and does a lot of good in her own way."

"Well," Pep said. "All's well that ends well. Good luck with Habitat."

Pep wandered off. Mom wheeled two wreaths and a box of Christmas ornaments toward the register. I don't generally lie, so I used what little money I had on three tubs of spackling compound I could donate to Habitat for Humanity, as soon as I got their address.

and i found myself thinking about her

I remembered my Grandma Pearl's death from cancer, and how afterward I could recall her only as she was in the hospital. The hospital room doorway was the museum frame that held her image, until one day she came back to me, running water over a package of frozen strawberries. Do you choose the way you remember someone? No, you remember them the last way you saw them, until you make that go away and replace it with something else. And so, when I felt ready, I went to the main lobby at the end of a school day, when all the buses had left. I stood in front of the trophy case.

111.

below sea level

When I first met Jenney on the phone, I didn't look for her trophy because I didn't think I should find out facts she didn't tell me, including her last name. If I happened to be in this part of the building, I would rush by so that I wouldn't even be tempted. But now, I decided, I would find her award—and this hallway, not the cemetery, would be the place where I'd remember Jenney.

It's funny how trophies show an idealized world. The first trophy case was like a miniature city with everyone living in penthouses. Bronze guys and flamingo-legged girls all posed on top of gold and silver skyscrapers. Many of the trophies were for cheerleading, but the sculptor didn't get the pom-poms right. They looked solid and spherical, like basketballs with hair.

The second trophy case was full of plaques: wooden slabs like the kind steaks are served on, except that each slab held the outline of Massachusetts, rectangular on three sides, then hooking south onto Cape Cod and falling into disorder in the water. I wasn't sure which sport these were for.

Next I passed a row of signs:

PLAY LIKE A CHAMPION TODAY!

OFFENSE WINS GAMES. DEFENSE WINS CHAMPIONSHIPS.

EXCELLENCE DOESN'T JUST HAPPEN—IT'S A DECISION YOU
MAKE EVERY DAY.

Around the corner I found the Schooners Hall of Fame. The name "Schooners" is great material for sportswriters: SCHOONERS BLOW BY [DEFEATED TEAM], SCHOONERS SAIL PAST [DEFEATED TEAM], SCHOONERS SAIL TO VICTORY, or even SCHOONERS TORPEDO [DEFEATED TEAM]. ("What an anachronism," Mom tsked.) Of course, the metaphors don't work with some opponents' names: SCHOONERS SAIL PAST PANTHERS. HORNETS STING SCHOONERS.

A new reporter tried to rename the girls' teams Schoonerettes, but the girls and their mothers mounted a protest. My mom, who generally ignores organized sports, wrote a letter saying that all boats and ships are female anyway, so shouldn't it be the boys' teams that change their name? The "-ettes" name vanished, as did the reporter.

"That's right, go," Mom said when his departure was announced in the newspaper. "Run off with your tail between your legs."

The Schooners Hall of Fame, I saw, was created in 1954. The first Hall of Famers were all male, clean-cut guys in checked jackets who looked forty but were probably eighteen. Division champions, MVPs, in multiple sports, of course—one for each season, because God forbid you should have time on your hands. Go-getters, every one. Beyond the Hall of Fame stood a case of miscellaneous awards: a leather football helmet old enough for the Brooksbie, some ribbons faded from ivory to gray, and three plaques with combinations of urns, scrolls, and laurel leaves that you would never see in nature. One of them said:

NORTH OF BOSTON SCHOLAR-ATHLETE OF THE YEAR

2009–2010

JENNEFER ALVES

HAWTHORNE HIGH SCHOOL

Sponsored by

Schneider Lumber

The *Hawthorne Beacon-Times*

Radio Station WSEA

Outside the school, two massive flagpoles had nothing to wave. Identical benches of local granite, given as a class gift each year, swarmed the front door like tombstones in a crowded cemetery. Couldn't one class come up with something new, like a birdbath or a hitching post?

I unlocked Triumph from the bike rack and looked across the frozen mud of the football field.

There's an empty chair here waiting for you.

There is?

For when you decide to come here and volunteer. Right next to me.

I thought the worst part of losing Jenney would be feeling responsible for her death. It wasn't. A whole other kind of sadness waited for me: knowing that the future I imagined was not going to happen. Meeting her in person. Introducing her to my parents. Her beside me at Listeners, where we would graduate to overnights and race in the chairs. Her death and the end of my plans were related. It took a long time for my mind to accept that.

She was a girl talking to me in the dark. The first one. A darkness I created myself by closing my eyes. But still.

Jenney, I'm back outside by my bike now. I'll lift Triumph from the bike rack, snap my helmet on, adjust my pack, swing my leg over the saddle, and schoon along. Then I'll try an old route backward, or a new route forward. Two years from now I'll leave for college, four years later for graduate school, and almost no one will remember the things we told each other.

But enough about me.